Water
Weal

PAMELA ST ABBS

DEDICATION

Joyce, Pauline, Charles and Dolly

CONTENTS

Acknowledgement

With thanks to Bill for all his support.

Chapter 1

Mrs Maggie Norrice saw the car in the river. The early evening mist had been driven from the water by a firm breeze. Waves were moving from the car, hitting the banks and going back towards the vehicle sinking into the depths of the River Sparrow. The returning waves hit outward going ones making the water stew.

The dew soaked through her brown nylon trousers as she crouched in the long grass and she was grateful for her small size. She tried to wrap her pink cardigan around her. It tore where her fingers pulled it. She may be a bit over seventy but she felt much older tonight. The dampness had even seeped into her two pairs of socks. It seemed strange that the grass should be so wet when the weather had been hot and sunny for weeks.

But these things didn't matter. There was a man standing on the bridge examining the break in the railings, which the car had fallen through. He made a broad, tall silhouette against the moon. A cat sprang along the bridge past him. The man took a swipe at it. It let out a wail, swung tip and tail away and scuttered for the safety of the bank.

Maggie barely noticed her favourite cat's narrow escape for she had seen the water take another life. And the torturous fluid was already settling back over the car. Now she saw, in the place where the car had splashed into the river, an image of a drowning man. It was not the man from the car. This was a picture from her past that had come to live with her. It was an old memory, coming to her less often in the last twenty years, but the sight of the sinking car had rent this form from the depths of her mind.

She saw the still face just below the surface of the water, which, in her mind, had changed to ice. The pallid features were more than familiar; they were part of her, mingled in her blood. It was her father's face. It broke through, scattering shards of ice, cleared the surface and taunted Maggie to remember.

She could not forget. She could never forget. Her mind was frozen into her past.

The wood and metal drummed with the sound of running on the bridge bringing Maggie back to her present situation. Without realising it she'd worked her way up to the top of the bank, level with The Wet Goose public house. Two of her cats mewed at her as they stalked the June grass. Her knees ached from squatting so long. She knew she would have to get by the broken bridge to get back home. Perhaps the village side of the bank might be safer, but no: lights had started to come on, and as the man from the bridge ran along the road past the pub he triggered a security light. It hurt her eyes. He turned.

Had he heard her? Had he seen her?

She saw his face.

For Maggie this was the face to fear. It was the face of murder, evil and villainy. Yet to her it was also the most beautiful face in all the world with its strong even features and smooth fair skin. Once she had loved such a face, lusted for the owner of such a face. She wished she had not seen it for she guessed her father's ghost had created such a daemon to drive her to suicide. But she had decided many years ago she would not give him that pleasure.

Chapter 2

Kinera Kran saw Maggie Norrice from her window. These studio lights built into one side of her attic room reached above the level of the bank. They gave her a view of the river and Mrs Norrice's house the other side.

She hoped her little notes to the old woman had upset her. Maggie Norrice snooped; everyone knew it, so why didn't people complain about her, wondered Kinera.

Pulling away, she caught her own reflection in the glass. Her own outline framed Maggie Norrice's house. The locket she always wore hung in line with the door. She could see there was too much grey in her hair for her forty years. She didn't like the way the grey had appeared in tufts among her chestnut curls. Ordinarily she couldn't care less how she looked, but it surprised her tonight to see how worn her grey eyes looked and how leathery her face. She touched her lips. They felt dry, but so did her fingers.

She'd heard a mighty splash in the river. It had brought her to the window. She lit a cigarette and enjoyed the thought of the filthy smoke penetrating her lungs and circulating in her body.

On the far bank Maggie Norrice was scrambling up the bank from the river. There were small movements around her where cats bounced over and through the long grass towards her house. Kinera hated that house in the same way she hated Maggie Norrice and the whole village. She felt it was part of a conspiracy to prevent nature's will. The river's high banks and sluices were to keep the river in its place. The electric pumping station up stream was there to lift the water from the land drains and put it in the river. But it was the history of that conspiracy that she hated most. The fight against the will of the water had been going on so long. And that's what Maggie Norrice's house represented. The cut down wind-pump, painted black, where the old woman lived, stood next to the fine Victorian architecture of the steam pump house with its tall chimney stack.

Going back further was the church, placed on the highest of the low lying ground; it had been built with a separate tower to allow the flood waters to flow around it without hindrance.

Kinera poured a glass of gin and drank it. She called Maggie Norrice a 'Silly Cow,' and heard a tap on the door.

The light from the hallway shone on the body of a sleek, athletic young woman as she stood naked by the door. Her skin, coloured from her south European roots glowed; her straight black hair shone white where it caught the harsh beam of the light bulb behind her.

'Do you have to scrabble at the door like a ruddy mouse, Bon,' said Kinera.

'I heard something, a splash,' said Bonita. The naked woman's Spanish accent lulled the words.

'A car's gone in the river,' Kinera snapped.

'Shall I call the police?'

'No, Bon, lights are coming on all over the village, someone else will have done it.' Kinera looked at her with her face screwed into a fist. 'Go to bed. Leave me alone,' she yelled.

'All right, all right. Please don't shout. You know I can't stand it.' The young woman turned away, the borrowed light cutting a changing silhouette as she moved. The lines were slender, but soft and smooth.

'I'm sorry, Bonita.'

'Goodnight, Kin.'

'Goodnight, Bon.'

Being alone with her misery -- that's what she liked best. Bonita had gone and shut the door. Kinera stubbed her cigarette out on the windowpane where it lined up with Maggie Norrice's bedroom window.

The light was on there now. She could see the yellow glow through a crack in the dark curtains. What was she up to shut up in that house all day only creeping out with her cats at night?

She turned to her paintings, just shadows in the corner. It pleased her to distort daffodil fields with craters and darken fields of ripe corn. With the lights out her pictures were nothing, like sleeping children.

Tears came into her eyes like grime.

'Am I the only one who cares if he's dead?' she shouted, suddenly drawn again to the window, this time by the call of police sirens.

'Kin?' said Bonita. Kinera looked up: she'd returned.

The young woman's voice bathed Kinera for a moment and she

folded, her shoulders touching her knees.

'I knew you were upset.'

Kinera thought for a moment that Bonita sounded pleased she'd been right, but the girl embraced her and she was grateful for the comfort. 'I hate this place,' she said.

'It's just the accident with the car,' said Bonita. 'It's frightened you.'

She felt she was being cajoled so Kinera snapped, 'No, it hasn't. I feel nothing.'

'You feel everything,' said Bonita.

'I want to phone Ken,' said Kinera.

'Not tonight, not now. You are divorced. He is no longer your husband.' Bonita's voice made those harsh words sound a kindness. Kinera cried with Bonita holding her.

Campbell watched water gush from the car on the bank and realised the rescuers had nothing to rescue. The only occupant of the car was already dead. Parnold stood beside Campbell, taller younger, physically more solid and stronger than himself. An ancient Dane had no doubt given him his colouring in the same way some French blood had given him his own hooknose and sallow skin, mused Campbell. But he knew their inner strengths were always in control. Neither man spoke in the greyness before dawn.

The breeze got up and, channelled between the riverbanks, it was almost a wind. Campbell felt it move his short brown hair and cut around his fleshless legs. It tugged at his black raincoat where his bony hands sheltered in the pockets. It would be hot later, but plucked from his bed he felt chilled. He looked at the body still in the driver's seat of the car. The pathologist was examining the dead man.

Gathering up his gangly arms and legs he went across and hunched himself down by the car. For him there was little revulsion at the physical changes of the body caused by its death, but they signalled the end of a person just a little older than himself. He felt a distant grief, a sorrow at the loss of life and a loneliness as the one to resolve the mystery of the man's death.

'You wouldn't know it was the beginning of June,' said Campbell to the pathologist. Such a statement seemed to sum up the situation to Campbell but the doctor looked at him as if he hadn't understood his Edinburgh accent.

'I think I recognise him,' said Parnold from over Campbell's shoulder. Campbell moved out of his way. He thought he heard him say something about Scotsmen and decided not to take it personally as the bank allowed him to still see into the car in his new position.

The victim was a broad man who filled the area allowed for the driver even with the seat adjusted as far back as it would go. His white hair was receding from a square brow, which was creased and bruised in a line across it. The rest of his face was heavy, small featured and unmarked.

He mentioned it to the pathologist who told him the victim could have caught his face on the steering wheel, but he wouldn't be sure until he'd completed the post mortem.

'It's Graham Pleasance,' said Parnold. 'He left the police force about three years ago and went to work for the refuse disposal authority. He had to control what went on at the rubbish tip. I remember him telling me.'

'Before my time here,' said Campbell.

The man's identity card for his work and his driving licence were found on him, confirming these facts, and the body was removed from the car. His pockets further yielded the usual items of everyday life: handkerchief, wallet and small change. The interior of the car was unremarkable also. The automatic gear lever was in drive, the ignition key was in its slot in the steering column in the "on" position, and the windows were closed.

Campbell withdrew to the bridge where a pair of uniformed colleagues was measuring distances along the road and the gap in the railings, which the car had passed through.

But his mind was still occupied with the meeting yesterday, though he didn't know why he couldn't dismiss the whole thing. All that management consultant had talked about throughout the day was how to measure work: listing numbers of visits, the time spent on such jobs as answering the phone – this in addition to their normal reports. He'd told the man if they stopped talking about measuring the job, he could get on and do it. But no one had listened. They'd smiled at him as if he wasn't in their club. The club of management speak and those who didn't like real work, he thought. He had recognised some of their young faces, promoted out of the way because they were unable to cope with the realities of policing.

He wondered how anyone could measure the thought patterns in his brain. The very brain functions that told him this car draining on the bank next to the crane had not fallen into the river by accident.

The sky was lightening. Yellow and white light trickled along the edge of the low horizon and filtered across the misted sky. The first aircraft of the day from the local American airbase roared through the cloudless sky on its way to the bombing range on the Wash. Ducking from the noise Campbell noticed the sign at the edge of the bridge. He walked down the steep ramp to read it.

"Private. Use at your own risk." The bridge looked stout enough to him with its iron framework and thick wooden boarding. 'Any thoughts?' he asked one of the measuring policemen.

'There are no skid marks, Sir,' he replied. 'He couldn't have been travelling very fast because the car fell only just beyond the bridge. There's very little flow in these inland fen rivers, until the sluices are opened up when the tide starts to run out. So it stayed very much where it was.'

Campbell noted that the bridge was at right angles to the road. The car would have had to turn sharply to get on the bridge and, if it had been going fast, it would have had trouble doing that. Before the bridge a closed metal gate marked the entrance to a hard band of orange, flattened sand and hard-core which formed an access road labelled, "Ouseland River Authority, Authorised vehicles only." Surely the driver would have preferred to crash into that than risk the river? And there was no sign of braking or swerving, nor was the car badly damaged, which it would have been if it had smashed into the bridge with any force.

Yes, he'd absorbed that information without realising it. That was why it was not an accident. The only statistic he cared about now was solving this one case. He decided that those counting his efficiency could go and count strawberry plants if they wanted. They would not interfere with his investigations.

From the centre of the bridge Campbell surveyed the view to the north of the strip of narrow slate coloured road running in a straight line from the flat skyline of the fens. It met the riverbank head on, turned and ran along it before turning again and forming the bridge beneath his feet. The orange Ouseland River Authority road continued along the bank. He noted that this would take just one lorry going in one direction at a time, as a narrow but steep ditch on the other side of the track did not allow for pulling over. He could just see the top of the sluice, marking where this small river joined the larger tidal river on its way out to the Wash. He rocked forwards onto the balls of his feet and back on his heels. He turned. In the other direction the road from the bridge immediately turned two right angle bends by the Wet Goose Public House and then made a sweeping loop around the village before going south across level fields in a straight line to the horizon. Beside this stretch ran a ditch which had a couple of flat concrete bridges leading to farms.

The different crops produced ribbons of different shades of green and textures from the angle of the early sun. Poppies reddened along the edges of the un-ripened cornfields. This village was isolated – just one road and a few tracks. There were a few cottages with the church inside the loop of the southern half of the road and several houses clustered around the river. Someone here had to know something about last night.

When Parnold strode up to him he was reading the two other boards he'd found on the river bank: one told him it was the River Sparrow, the other told him the fishing rights belonged to a certain local fishing club. The young sergeant muttered something in a strong local accent about disliking the fens and then he asked Campbell whether he was going to see the victim's wife, Mrs Pleasance.

From Parnold's face he could tell the younger man did not wish to give the news of a loved one's death to someone he knew.

'Aye,' said Campbell. He recalled his first visit to the Fens. It had been his honeymoon. He had been fascinated then as he was now by the diverted rivers, dykes, new rivers and sluices used to control the water on the fens of the Wash. That huge drainage sink of land between the hump on the English map depicting East Anglia and England's straight eastern edge, Lincolnshire. It meant the land was only there because of human energy and creativity. It was shaped by them. The fields were rectangular, the dykes and roads straight, the crops were drilled in rows and only planted trees grew, as wind breaks. It was orderly, but he knew it was the water that drew him, gurgling along a viaduct or hidden from idle gaze beyond high banks or lying still and deep and dark in wide drainage channels. When he'd first moved this way he'd spent some time looking into the history of the fens.

Standing on the bridge he could see that the ordinary level of the River Sparrow was higher than the level of the fields. He knew the peaty soil was still shrinking from being drained. This could leave house owners having to build an extra step to their front door. It could also cause houses to lilt until they had to be abandoned.

And he could also see Mary Brown's forensic team going about their business of looking for the signs left behind by any human as surely as a snail leaves a trail of slime.

Parnold coughed.

'Aye, we must go and see the widow,' said Campbell with a sigh. How strange it was that he should start being interested in someone's life only when they were no longer living. Yet the life of Graham Pleasance would reveal the cause for his death. And that was what he was here for.

CHAPTER 3

Maggie Norrice turned off her bedroom light and undid the buttons of her pink cardigan. She didn't need the glaring bulb any more as sunshine was finding its way through her grimy window and the gap in her curtains. She hadn't bothered to watch the police go about their business because all she could see was the drowning face of her father, despite the sixty years since his death.

She didn't even know if the man in the car tonight was dead, though she guessed he was.

Her mind fell back more easily on the past than it gripped the present. She turned the pages of the scrapbook. Her father's young face beamed from the pages of yellowed newspaper clippings. She hadn't meant to kill him. How often had she told herself that? It always sounded like a lie.

The picture showed him with a shock of black hair, like her own had been before it had turned white. Even his dark eyes could have been hers. He must have been barely twenty then, before the time of wife and daughter. His smile was full of the joy of victory. One hand held a pair of ice-skates and the other a silver cup.

How could she have hated him so much? He had been the showman, the joker, the storyteller. He had often stood at the bar of the local pub telling of the days of fen skaters, bets, rivalries and, most of all, winning. Was any of that man left when he died?

Oh, these questions. She'd asked them of herself so many times before, but they didn't lay his memory. As she closed her eyes and fell back on her frail quilt her cats joined her for a daytime sleep. The light of the day would keep his drowning image from her, but she still dreamt of ice skates cutting, turning and tearing at the ice covering the frozen fields.

She turned, felt cold and drew his quilt about her.

Ruth Pleasance visibly shook when Campbell told her of her husband's death. He watched WPC Garden's frizzy brown mass of hair, squeezed out at the back of her hat in an non-regulation frothy pony tail, bob in front of him as she placed sugared tea before the victim's wife and wrap a blanket about her shoulders. Then Campbell sent the policewoman to phone for the woman's daughter.

Campbell absorbed the room. There was a lace doily underneath each ornament on the teak units. The cream carpet was deep and soft from frequent cleaning. A clean pastel pink and green mat decorated the middle of the room. He tried not to be comfortable in a pale pink velour armchair.

Garden came back and said, 'Miss Christine Pleasance will be here in about an hour. She's got to travel from Cambridge.'

Ruth Pleasance's carefully curled hair bobbed down as she wiped her small nose. She held the tissue on her cream coloured lap and flattened her skirt with her other hand. Her fingers trembled.

As he'd already decided she was too shaken to question in any depth he rose to leave, but she grabbed his arm.

'Are you sure it was him? He never goes that way,' she said.

'I've shown you his things,' said Campbell frowning, 'and my sergeant did know him. We will need you to confirm his identity as soon as you are ready.' He repeated this information he'd given earlier as if it was the first time he'd said it.

'I know it's a short cut home, but he prefers to go by the main road because of that awful bridge.' Her weak voice was trying to be demanding and the result, Campbell decided, sounded like a raving crow. But he looked closer. There was a strength behind her wet blue eyes.

While she was open to him he asked her, 'Was your husband working on anything he was concerned about, Mrs Pleasance?'

'You said you thought it was an accident?'

'No, I didn't,' corrected Campbell. 'I said he'd come off the bridge at Sparrow Bank. I said nothing about the cause, Mrs Pleasance.' She sunk back in her seat. 'It certainly looked like an accident,' he continued, 'but there were no signs of the car trying to stop or avoid the bridge.'

He let his words reach her, then he asked, 'Was he depressed in any way?'

'He was very involved with his work, Inspector,' said Ruth Pleasance, 'but not depressed.' She glanced up at a family picture framed in silver on the mantelpiece: a husband, wife and daughter. 'I love him,' she said. Her voice seemed to come from a dreamland inside her head, but it jolted her body. She started to choke and WPC Garden's soft, freckled hand rubbed the woman's back until she was able to catch her breath.

Campbell noted the present tense understanding that love didn't die as easily as people. He wondered how far he could question her this morning; he had already got further than he had expected to.

'May I have a picture of your husband, Mrs Pleasance,' he asked. She took down a portrait of Graham Pleasance placed next to the family one. Having passed it to Garden he leaned forward and said quietly, 'This sort of thing sometimes happens when the driver has been drinking.'

'My husband doesn't, didn't, drink, Inspector. Tea and coffee that's all he ever had.' Ruth Pleasance began to look blue around the lips.

'Shall we send for your doctor, Mrs Pleasance?' asked Campbell. She nodded so he sent Garden to the phone again. Any further questioning would have to wait.

To get any sort of picture of last night's events he knew he would have to look elsewhere. He would have to return to Sparrow Bank.

The heat of the morning had worked its way through Janet Sparrow's limbs. It had collected in her feet and in the ample creases of her body. The weight of her breasts created a thick line of sweat, which, she hoped, went unnoticed to anyone who saw her on her post round. But she still felt the discomfort from there more than from any other of her hot places.

She propped her bicycle against the blackened yellow brickwork of the Victorian engine house and walked across the yard to her older cousin's back door.

'Aunt Maggie, I've come with your pension,' she called. Because of the nearly forty years age difference she'd always been known as Auntie to her. As usual there was no reply. 'Auntie, I've brought cat food too.' There was a further silence. 'I'll leave it inside the old engine house as usual, shall I?'

She wanted her to come to the door and speak to her. They hadn't spoken for years. Occasionally she'd see a grey net curtain move, but no words. Oh well, if that was the way she wanted to live that was up to her, she thought. And then she corrected herself. 'Not today.' She said it out loud. Things were different since the drowning.

'I know you saw something last night. I know you go out at night with your cats. If you saw something you ought to tell the police. Auntie?'

She stood back and looked up at the converted wind pump with its timbered first floor and corrugated iron roof. Even as a child the house had seemed small. She remembered coming here once when she was eleven. It was then she'd started getting Auntie's shopping.

The layout of the place was simple enough. The back door opened onto a scullery. There was a bath plumbed in on the far side with a board over it, so it could be used as a table when not it in use, and there were shelves filled with all sorts of junk on the back wall. The far door led to the only other room on the ground floor, the living room. A black range was built in along one of its angled sides with a knotted rag rug in front of it.

She'd only been in that one time, but she recalled it clearly. It hadn't been as clean and tidy as her mother's house and as a child she'd liked that, but she guessed it was far dirtier now.

That day one of Auntie's cats had crept up the open staircase and called to Janet from the small triangular landing. A little thrill had fluttered in her chest as she'd followed it up the steep open steps.

There were two doors off the landing. The cat had wanted her to open the one on the right. It revealed an iron bed nearly filling the room. There had been three cats already asleep on the patchwork cover and the one she'd followed joined them. The bed left only enough room for a dressing table against the sloping walls; and on that she'd seen an old wedding photograph next to a picture of Auntie Maggie's father skating on the frozen wash lands.

Auntie had called her.

And now she wondered if she hadn't offered to do her shopping for her all those years ago – after all she wasn't old then – whether she would be a recluse now.

'Auntie, please talk to me,' she called at the door again. There seemed no reason for her to feel like this, so why was she so scared for her aunt?

As she left she thought she saw the bedroom curtain twitch, but she couldn't be sure.

Janet scooted a few yards down the track before mounting her bicycle and riding steadily to the road. At the pub Mrs Sturning, the landlady, was unlocking the front door. She didn't like the woman's bleached yellow hair and her harsh voice, and she wasn't local.

Anyway, Janet was irritable. It wasn't just her aunt that was worrying her. All the post had been delivered first thing and it wasn't until she'd been getting Auntie Maggie's pension and cat food back at the post office that she'd noticed an envelope tucked at the bottom of the post bag.

It had been then that this strange Scottish Police Inspector had shown her the photo. He'd just been in the post office himself. She guessed the picture was of the man in the car last night, but she didn't say so. The odd thing was she'd seen the dead man before, and she'd told the Inspector so. 'I'd been delivering the post to Drain Farm last week when I'd seen him and a Chinese girl out in the fields in front of the old barn.' She'd even gone to the trouble of showing him and his Sergeant the location of it on their map. But it had made her even later with this letter.

She was relieved, though, to see the police had been quick to put the bridge back into use. The river divided the village and the only other way round to the other bank was a five-mile trip. They'd screened off the section where the car'd gone through last night, and even a small car wouldn't get past it now, but it was no trouble for her with her bike.

She couldn't pedal up the side of the bridge anyway, it was too steep. So she dismounted and walked her bike up it. She could hear police moving about behind the screening. She wondered at all the activity; surely it had always been an accident waiting to happen?

Making herself turn her back to it, Janet looked at the view. She liked sharing the name of the river. The Sparrow was silent this morning just a breeze moving over it. There was no noticeable flow and she guessed the sluice at the end was closed to prevent the sea pushing up the river on its incoming tide.

A 'Can you move on, please,' from a uniformed policeman took her by surprise. She nodded and turned from the river. She'd always felt it too reckless to ride down the slope of the bridge with the road turning immediately to the right at the bottom. She really didn't fancy falling into the hawthorn hedge that marked the boundary of the holiday cottage there. And occasionally a heavy lorry would pull across to the yellow gate at the end of the Ouseland River Authority road that led down to the sluice without the driver looking towards the bridge.

She turned in the opposite direction at the base of the bridge, away from the sandy lane of the river authority track, and followed the main tarmac road next to the river. She barely noticed the height of the bank above her. It had always been there and she expected it always would be. The road turned away from the river and Janet's path became a track as she made her way to Kinera Kran's house.

She didn't like her either, nor her Spanish friend. There was something odd about people who spent all their days painting pictures. But she still felt she had to knock and apologise for the letter being late.

While she waited she turned the neat white envelope about in her square hands. Mrs Kran was always getting official sort of post and she was always in the post office buying stamps. She knew it was none of her business but she would have liked to know why all the same.

The door opened. It was Mrs Kran.

'Reading people's post again,' she said.

'I don't,' said Janet. She noticed Mrs Kran's slurred speech and forgot to apologise for the letter's lateness. Instead, she thrust it into the woman's painty hands.

'You're just as friendly as your aunt,' said Mrs Kran. 'I know what she's up to, you know. I now she spies on folk. Don't you worry the police will get her.'

'My aunt's a good woman, better than you'll ever be,' said Janet pulling her bicycle from the hedge where she'd left it. Aunt Maggie wasn't exactly an Aunt, more of a cousin. Maggie's father and Janet's grandfather had been brothers. And she wondered if Maggie was a good woman. 'She's still family,' she muttered.

Chapter 4

The white painted frontage of The Wet Goose Public House glared at Campbell. He'd just turned around from leaving his jacket in the car having taken his notebook from its pocket. He was annoyed that no one was in at Drain Farm, where the post woman had seen Graham Pleasance with a Chinese girl. He tried to dismiss his unease by writing Janet Sparrow's information into his notebook. Parnold shuffled his feet next to him.

Shielding his eyes with his hand Campbell noted the cracks in the rendering on the pub's walls and the lack of paint on the woodwork. There were no tubs of flowers and no hanging baskets. A chalkboard declared the place open and the outer door was ajar. He read the words above it; they declared the licensee to be Mrs Elizabeth Mary Sturning.

There was no bar tender, and just one customer sat in the only bar. This aged man didn't turn from his pint of beer or stop smoking his thin, self-rolled cigarette when he and Parnold came in.

The room was cool and dark. An American bomber aircraft passed over head so Campbell waited until he could focus on the man's veined eyes.

It was as if Parnold hadn't seen the notice above the door, thought Campbell, as his colleague banged on the bar and shouted, 'Landlady'.

There was no reply. Eventually the customer said, 'She's out back,' without taking his cigarette from the corner of his mouth.

Campbell left Parnold in the bar in case the man was mistaken and took a back door. Instead of finding himself in a garden with tables and chairs he found he was in a roughly concreted yard. On one side there was a kitchen extension sandwiched between the main building and a larger brick barn. On his other side was the wall of the flat roofed toilet block, which enclosed the area by joining on to the barn at one end and the main building at the other.

He could see the person he guessed to be the landlady, Mrs Sturning, standing by the kitchen window busy at the sink. Her round face was painted white with make-up and her eyes had a rainbow of colours over them. On top she wore a crest of spiky yellow hair which became suddenly dark where it was rooted to her head. It took him a moment to take this in, then he hailed her with a raised hand and an, 'Ah, hello.' It sounded very Scottish, even to him.

As he saw her look up, he heard a low growl beside him. The breath of the dog that had made the sound moved his trousers so the fabric touched his leg. He turned to face the black and tan dog, making a gesture to the woman to get her to call the animal away. He didn't want to shout in case the dog took this to be the sign of an enemy and attack.

He told the dog to sit, but it did not budge. It stood with barred teeth within centimetres of his skin. Campbell took a pace backwards. The dog took the space he had left. He could feel himself moving into the corner of the yard between the barn and the kitchen extension. While he looked at the saliva drivelling from its jaws he wondered whether the dog would respond to 'Hello' or 'Down' in the same way as it had to 'Sit'.

Mrs Sturning appeared at a door next to her kitchen window. It seemed a long way to Campbell though it could only have been a couple of yards. His arms felt vulnerable without his jacket.

She nodded when Campbell queried her name, 'Mrs Sturning?'

'He doesn't like policemen,' she said. Campbell raised his eyebrows and watched the flash of realisation on her face at how bad that sounded. She smiled, but did nothing to call off her dog. 'We've had some break-ins recently. They've made the dog nervous, and each time a copper came round.'

Her accent, he decided, was not local. She was one of those people who would deny coming from London yet had spent most of her life no further north than Hounslow. And that was probably most of her thirty years.

'I daren't try and pull him off,' Mrs Sturning continued. 'I'll get some chocolates. He'll let you out then.'

It was hard keeping his stance neutral while the animal still growled at him in the corner. He watched Mrs Sturning go through the door he'd used from the bar. Her sling backs flapped from the straps being trodden down underneath her heals.

WDC Jenner almost immediately replaced her. He could see she was trying not to smile but her clear blue eyes gave her away, and this irritated him. But he wanted to keep still and give the dog no information as to his state of mind. He would not even admit how he felt to himself.

The dog moved back slightly. Campbell noticed a bunching of muscles around its shoulders. He thought it was going to attack. Instead it turned and fled through the kitchen door-way.

Campbell looked at Jenner – impeccable in her short sleeved suit and tightly pleated hair despite the weather. She took her hand out of her pocket and brandished a small cylindrical device.

'Dog scarer,' she explained tilting her blond head. 'I like dogs. It doesn't really harm them,' and she put it away.

'Thank you,' said Campbell making sure there was enough finality in his voice to change the subject and to hide his relief. He was grateful to see Parnold coming out of the pub with Mrs Sturning.

'Where's the dog?' asked Mrs Sturning.

'In the kitchen,' said Jenner.

'Thank you,' said Campbell – this time dismissing his rescuer.

'I came to give you a message. This was left under the windscreen of one of the police cars.' Jenner passed the paper to him, already bagged in a clear evidence bag so he could still read it, and left.

Campbell didn't want to read it in front of Mrs Sturning so he put it in his trouser pocket.

'Mrs Sturning, did you see anything last night?' asked Parnold. Campbell decided to watch this interview. Parnold looked clean and crisp in his white shirt and traditional yet modern tie. He somehow contrasted suitably with Mrs Elizabeth Sturning's bright bangles and short black skirt.

'I didn't see much but I heard the car splash into the river. I knew it would happen one day,' she said. 'I looked out of the window, but the riverbank is higher than the building. I can't even see the bridge – we're set too far back. But I still looked out. Funny isn't it?'

'Were there any other noises which were unusual?' asked Parnold. Campbell leaned forward slightly.

'No,' said Mrs Sturning. 'I'd've heard anything though. I've been so jumpy since the break-ins. Come to think of it, I thought I heard a car down old Maggie Norrice's lane opposite. Couldn't have been her though, she hasn't got a car. My husband said I must've been imagining things.'

'Where is Mr Sturning?' asked Parnold.

'He's gone up the shops. He took me kids to school and then he's gone to the cash and carry. He wouldn't have heard anything anyway. He sleeps like he's dead every night. I sent him down to check the doors. He said to me he didn't see anything. You can ask him when he gets back if you like.'

Campbell wondered at the speed she spoke and if her mind was as quick as her tongue, or could it just be that she spoke without thinking?

'And that mutt's meant to be a guard dog,' she continued. 'And yet he lets in house breakers. I've got me two kids here. I thought you police would be able to do something about all this.'

Parnold twitched irritably and opened his mouth, but Campbell spoke, 'Security is quite a problem these days. Have you spoken to our Crime Prevention Officer?' He raised his eyebrows, hunched his shoulders and brought his hand up to brace his chin.

Having mumbled something about yet more expense Mrs Sturning said, 'There's no money in the business anyway. We're thinking of getting out. It's no place for the kids, and it's them what's important, ain't it?'

Campbell shifted his weight slightly. She seemed to take this as agreement and smiled. He decided it was time to show her the picture of Graham Pleasance. He took it out of his pocket and asked her if she'd seen him before.

She made a nasal sound of recognition. 'Been in here a couple of lunch times last week with a Chinese girl. Don't really know either of them though, but we don't get a lot of lunchtime trade so I would remember them, 'specially with her being Chinese looking. Tuesday and Wednesday it was, one 'till two, on the dot. Always notice me old clock chime.'

'Was he here last night?'

'I wouldn't know who was in the bar last night. My husband was doing the bar. I was in the kitchen doing the food.'

'Thank you, madam,' said Campbell. The woman didn't seem able to give any more information, so it was time to leave and read the note Jenner had given him. Then he would see about the Chinese girl.

'Only a splash, Sergeant Parnold,' Campbell muttered as he walked up to the bridge, the note in one hand. He touched the heavy iron framework forming the span and the sturdy timbers used along the sides with his other hand. A car would have to be going very fast to break through such a barrier.

Having reached the canvas screening, he opened a flap and saw one of Mary Brown's photographers busy taking pictures of the place where the car had gone through the side of the bridge.

'Don't touch,' snapped Mary from behind him.

He was already shoving his hands in to his pockets as she spoke. Her ample bosom almost touched him when he turned to her, so he took a pace to the side.

She'd elbowed Parnold out of the way and was peering at the lengths of timber still attached to the bridge as she continued, 'It was taken down. My dear, I don't like to say it but my predecessor would never have noticed it. Look at the holes in the wood where the bolts were and the inside of the nuts. They've been smoothed. The car would have gone through even if it had only been pushed.'

'Couldn't that have been caused by the bolts ripping through them?' asked Campbell.

'Possibly, but look.' Mary Brown pointed to scoring around the edges of one of the nuts and a mark on the heavy wooden planks.

'Just a splash,' said Campbell and he sucked his lower lip thoughtfully.

'No crash, just splash,' she agreed. She stood upright folding her arms beneath her ample breasts.

She was one of the few people who seemed able to make the same jumps of thought as he did. He smiled. She always made him feel like a small boy. Today he felt he had got ten out of ten for a spelling test. But her 'splash' had not only congratulated him, but dismissed him also. Her tone told him that she was busy and she was not going to tolerate Inspectors under her feet.

So he left her to it and looked up and down the river, he could just see the solid square top of the sluice where the River Sparrow joined the main tidal river. He turned about. In this direction he saw that only one house was tall enough to have a view of last night's events, and that was the tall thin building, just one room deep like a dolls house. But it was the studio windows built into the loft that gave it the height to survey the bridge and the river.

Campbell fingered the bagged note: Kinera Kran, River Farm. The name of the house he was looking at was printed in white letters by the gate. It matched the address on the head of the paper in his hand. He leaned back to balance as his feet slid down the grassy slope.

Parnold had taken himself off and was talking to a policewoman by Mary Brown's van. Campbell noted the young man's stance: his feet spread apart, his hips slightly forward. He called him twice. This was not a time for sex; an investigation was under way. He let his strong Scottish accent tell Parnold of his disapproval in the way he said his name.

Parnold knocked on Mrs Kinera Kran's door while Campbell stood near the gate and wondered at the design of fenland cottages. If he were to break down the shapes used in the houses everything would be a neat rectangle with one side being precisely twice the length of the other. From where he stood he could just see the studio lights in the roof. He hoped the people here had seen something. Note leavers were so often time wasters, and he had no time for side issues.

He moved forward when he heard the door open. A slender black-eyed woman stepped into the sunlight, her long black hair reflecting blue in the sun. Parnold introduced himself and Campbell as Police and the girl asked them in. Her Spanish accent gave Campbell a feeling of sympathy for her foreignness until he saw the way Parnold was looking at her. He decided it was fortunate the girl had her back to them, and he gave Parnold a warning look.

'My name is Bonita Arlotte. I am here to learn from Kinera Kran. She is such a great artist,' she said, swinging her hips beneath their flowered shorts. The slim gap of olive flesh between them and her top barely creased with the movement. 'Kinera sent me with the note. She is expecting you. I will get her. Sit.' She flapped her hands at wicker seats set around a wood burning stove.

'She has a fire all year. She feels the cold,' explained Bonita as she opened the door.

Campbell heard her espadrilled feet climbing the stairs shortly followed by an additional clatter of clogs coming down.

The clogged woman looked at him. He saw her tiredness under the brightly coloured scarf, which was twisted round her head like a turban allowing tufts of chestnut and grey hair to show at the sides. He saw a flash of misery in the way she wriggled her arms inside her painting smock. But her eyes moved on rapidly over the room. Campbell saw them rest on a pine chest where a carafe of clear liquid stood with a glass next to it. Under the glass was a letter. She went over to it, poured herself out a drink and moved the carafe and the letter to the windowsill so she could sit down on the chest.

Campbell explained as little as possible of the situation, he wanted her unaffected view of last night. 'I understand you have a good view of the river here, Mrs Kran,' he added conversationally.

'Only from my attic studio,' said Kinera. Campbell noted the strong perfume she wore. The air from the loose fitting casement window next to her brought the scent to him across the room. He also noted how tightly she gripped the edge of the chest she was sitting on.

'Did you see anything last night?' asked Parnold before Campbell had formed the same question.

'No,' said Kinera.

'And what about you?' Parnold asked of Bonita Arlotte.

Her simple negative answer left a silence in the room. Campbell began to fear that the note had been just a waste of time, as if they didn't have enough to do. He shook his head, no, he must try and get everything he could out of the interview.

'You know there was a man killed in the car that went off the bridge last night.' He relaxed into his chair and stretched his legs forward. 'I don't think it was an accident.'

'You think murder?' asked Bonita.

'Shut up, Bon' snapped Kinera Kran. 'Of course he means murder. What else could he mean? You don't have to shoot a man to kill him. You can be "criminally negligent". That's the phrase, isn't it? The garage can forget to put the brakes back correctly. In everybody's heart that is still murder, isn't it, Inspector?'

That hadn't been the sort of answer he'd expected or particularly wanted, so he looked at his feet.

'I'm sorry, Inspector,' said Bonita going to her friend. 'She had a very bad night.'

Campbell looked up. 'You sent me a note,' he said. 'You wanted to speak with me. What was it you wanted to say, Mrs Kran?'

Kinera Kran shook Bonita from her and said, 'That woman opposite saw what happened. I saw her coming back from her ramblings last night. She goes out prowling with her cats. She saw what happened. You must question her.'

'We will be talking to everyone in the village, Mrs Kran.' Campbell pulled out the picture of Graham Pleasance and passed it to her. 'Let me show you a picture.'

She took a while to look at it and think, sipping her drink as she did so. 'I remember that face. My husband and I used to have a beach hut years ago. He used to have one a bit further up the beach. We used to say "Hello" but he wasn't very friendly. His wife was one of these fussy sorts. He always had his daughter in tow – a great lanky thing. Like a boy. I haven't seen the man for years.' She handed back the picture and he passed it to Bonita.

'Oh, yes, I have,' she said. 'I've seen him at the pub two lunch times last week. Tuesday and Wednesday, I think. He was with a girl -- how you say? – from the east. She had long black hair, even straighter than mine, but tall: too tall to really be all Chinese.' She stopped, opened the stove doors and poked the fire.

'Thank you for your information,' said Campbell nodding to Parnold to leave quickly. He moved onto the edge of his seat and stood up. If only Parnold would stop gazing at the Spanish girl like that.

'Did the man in the car leave anyone behind?' asked Kinera Kran before they left the room.

'Yes, Mrs Kran. He left the grown-up daughter and the wife you met at the beach,' said Campbell.

'Poor cows,' she said realisation that Graham Pleasance was the dead man forming in her eyes. 'It was him in the picture?'

Campbell nodded in the knowledge that this information would be on the lunchtime news.

Bonita Arlotte followed them to the gate. Her soft voice brushed Campbell and Parnold apart. They looked at her.

'She's had a very sad life, Inspector, but she is a great artist. Her husband Kenneth adores her, you know, and she him. But they cannot live together. It is such a tragedy. And I cannot get out of them why they tear at each other like wild dogs.'

Once she'd gone in Campbell turned to Parnold and grumbled, 'Put your tongue away, it'll get gravel on it.

Chapter 5

Maggie Norrice was woken by someone knocking on the door. She'd heard her cousin, Janet, calling to her some time ago. She wondered if she'd come back. Sometimes she wanted to speak to the girl, though by now she was probably in her forties, not a girl at all. But she knew she could not start belonging to the outside world again. She did not deserve that.

But this time it was a man's voice. He kept saying he was the police and he would like to talk to her. She crept down stairs and sat on the bottom step looking at the scullery door. The man wasn't local, Scottish – she knew that much from the TV Janet had bought her. It stood in the corner of the living room perched on the top of an old table. She rarely turned it on.

This man was easy to shun. He would want to know the truth and despite all the evil in the face of the man on the bridge she could not surrender his identity.

Another man's voice, this time with a local accent, called to her. There was a harshness to it. It made her cover her ears with her ragged cardigan. She wanted to go back to her bedroom. She looked back up the staircase.

It was unchanged from the day her father found the tin.

Her father held her tin above his head. Flowers and pheasants decorated the container her mother had given her. It was the only thing of hers left.

The weather had been cold for months, frozen taps, ice willow patterns on the inside of the windows, frozen meadows and wash-lands, but no skates – not by then, not in this house anyway. She wondered where all the snow would go when the thick white blankets melted. The River

Sparrow and the drain the pump house served were frozen too. One night she'd heard a bang as the top sheet of river ice had been broken by another level of ice forming under it. The pressure of the expanding ice'd pushed at it until it had given way – so she'd been told later on. The pumps were silent, unable to pump ice. She missed the throb of the engines that she had never heard in all of her nearly sixteen years until they were still.

'You're just like her,' her father said that day. With her dark hair scratched back from her angular face she doubted that she looked like anything. He held the tin close to her face. 'Full of lust just like your mother.' (He had, of course, been right: not about her mother but about her. She knew that now, but then all she could think of was how often he had said such things.) She never thought of having a husband, being a wife, having a child. These were things women did. But her father said they did more.

He always said that her mother had been after airmen during the war, that her mother had liked men, any man, but him. He'd said it so often sitting by the range swilling dark bottles of strong smelling brew. But it could not be true, because his words burnt her inside.

'I in't,' she said, watching her tin. "Besides, I feel and look like a tramp in these scratchy old clothes," she thought and found herself saying, 'No man comes here that don't have to.' She saw hate flicker in his eyes. She needed that tin. 'Please don't take it. It's all I have.'

'You're not my child, you know that?'

'Please don't say that. You know I love you.'

'She'd been happy until you were inside her. She knew you weren't mine. When you were born she started to hate me.'

'That in't true. I was born afore the war. It can't be all my fault.' She saw his hand lift over her, still holding the tin. 'Please,' she wailed. His hand turned and he threw the tin to the floor. The lid rolled off and money spilled out.

'You've been stealing from me,' he demanded.

'I hin't, honest. I've been saving, that's all.'

'My money. All the money in this house is mine and don't you forget it.'

She wanted to scrabble down there and pick it up; instead she watched him put it in his pocket. It had been her escape money, and now it was gone.

'All you're going to do is drink that money away.' She almost spat the words at him.

'That has nothing to do with you. You have no right to tell me what I can or can't do.'

He stormed out of the house, and came home drunk, as usual. He slept for hours in front of the range.

She remembered the almost physical pain. How her temper had left her rattled. Why hadn't she been able to control it? But if she'd said nothing he would not have known how she felt. She remembered how it had taken hours for her body to stop shaking afterwards. She had known then that her outburst had been useless. He would not stop filling his body with poison.

Dreaming of her freedom had kept her going, looking at the horizon and living in a make believe world where she was someone else's child, lost in a wilderness. But when he'd taken her money…

'I wonder what happened to the tin?' said Maggie wrapping her holed pink cardigan around her. The cat she spoke to rubbed its head against her leg.

The policemen outside had stopped shouting.

Campbell moved away from the door. Maggie Norrice was not going to open up, not yet. He stretched his neck. There must be a way to get her to talk – it would come to him. He climbed the riverbank and looked down on her converted wind pump home and the old Victorian engine house next to it. The drain which it used to pump into the river must have been filled in, he decided, probably diverted.

There was no water yet he could almost hear the sound of ghost pumps rhythmically moving the water to a higher level. He looked along the river. In the distance he could just see a flat, square building. The new electric pump was servicing the diverted drain. But this Victorian building before him said something about the people who built it. It was built tall with arched doorways and windows, honouring their engineering ability and human ingenuity. He could feel the designers' and builders' pride. He turned away to look at the cool depths of the river running gently under the bridge on its long journey to the Ouse and the Wash -- a level quiet movement. Its patience appealed to him. That was how life should be.

Parnold interrupted his thoughts with, 'She's not coming out, or saying out.'

'Aye,' said Campbell, not taking his eyes from the river and wondering if it was the fens that had brought out Parnold's local accent.

It was time to find the tall Chinese girl, he decided as he noticed a police car coming down the lane. He was sure Maggie Norrice could help them if she wanted to. But now WDC Jenner had placed her car between him and Parnold, her blond French-pleated hair bobbing as she spoke. It was something about the victim's widow, Mrs Pleasance. Her daughter had been looking through documents, and she had found a paper she wanted to show them.

'The answer's not with this old bat,' said Parnold nodding at Maggie Norrice's door.

'Jenner, see if you can find this oriental girl Graham Pleasance was with, while we go and see his daughter.' Campbell made this sound as if he was in agreement with Parnold.

Christine Pleasance stood in the bungalow doorway – more her father's daughter than her mother's to look at. She'd responded to Garden's phone call earlier in the day, and Parnold checked her name with a formal greeting.

Campbell noted that Parnold just matched her height. He watched her broad strong face trying to look level and friendly over her grief. There was nothing timid in the way she held herself inside her shirt and jeans and when she invited them in her voice was firm and deep. She walked stiffly as she took them down the hall to her father's study. Campbell decided that this could be caused by her trying to contain her emotions. He glanced at Parnold for any sign of attraction. He saw none.

'You mentioned some papers, Miss Pleasance?' queried Campbell.

Inside her father's study Campbell watched Christine pleasance bring out a single sheet of paper from the veneered desk drawer and place it on the top. Her straight nut coloured hair, tied back with a fabric-covered elastic band swished past his face. She apologised and Campbell sat in the office style seat behind the desk. Parnold stood cramped against the single shelf of books, which went all the way around the room. From his more comfortable position Campbell looked at the titles. They were all books about her father's work.

'It was as much a way of life to him as a job,' said Christine Pleasance. 'I can't imagine why. I suppose he thought he was doing something for the environment. He thought he could change the world – but he couldn't. No one can.'

'He tried,' said Parnold lifting a police manual from the shelf.

'You knew him?' she asked.

'Yes,' said Parnold.

'I didn't,' said Campbell fearing that Miss Pleasance would stop talking.

'He would go looking for people dumping illegally at evenings and week-ends even when he wasn't paid for the hours he put in. When he wasn't doing that he would be out with children on clean-up campaigns.' Christine's face looked tight as she said these things. Campbell wondered if it was distaste for her father's work method or for her father or just because of withheld grief.

'Did he have any other duties, Miss Pleasance,' he asked.

'Yes, he had to make sure the dump was run properly. They're contractors up there and he had to keep an eye on them, make sure they didn't do anything they shouldn't.'

'You know a lot about your father's job, Miss Pleasance,' said Campbell.

'He was that sort of man, Inspector,' she replied. 'His excitement would spill out of him. He would talk about it all the time. He'd never been like that about police work.' Parnold was nodding his head in agreement. 'I have to say, though, that I haven't heard him speak about his work recently,' she added.

'Now these papers?' asked Campbell.

'I was looking for the insurance and mortgage documents. He had a second mortgage on this place; I didn't realise that.' She stopped, reddened and moved the sheet of paper towards Campbell. 'Here they are: they look like registration numbers. I wonder if he'd seen someone dumping and they got nasty?'

Campbell made no movement. In his view the murder had been calculated, but the motive was worth considering.

'Thank you, Miss Pleasance,' said Campbell. 'We will check it out.'

'My father could be rather foolish, Inspector. I know he would go out on his own, see people without telling anyone. He had an over-developed sense of justice and he thought he was indestructible like a character from the movies.'

'What were you doing last night?' asked Parnold.

'I was at my flat asleep,' she replied.

'Alone?'

'Yes.'

'You have a car?'

'Yes. What is all this about?' Christine Pleasance looked at Campbell.

'Just routine question, Miss Pleasance.' Campbell passed the sheet with the vehicle numbers to Parnold as he rose from his seat. He watched the sergeant nearly run down the corridor and out into the bright sunshine. Then he asked her if her father knew any oriental women.

'He might at work, Inspector, but not otherwise,' she replied. He could see her watching Parnold's contained energy as she spoke.

'Thank you again for your help.' Campbell walked across the shingle path behind his sergeant heading swiftly towards the car. 'The colt has bolted,' he complained to himself rolling his shoulders. Desks always made him feel cramped. The toys of technology were about to solve the mystery of the numbers without them having to go anywhere, and that annoyed him just a little. It was, after all, the first bit of really useful information they'd got so far.

But the car was too hot – the bungalow had been cool. His stomach churned at the thought of waiting inside the metal container for the computers to answer the history of the numbers. So he stood by the gate and looked at the cul-de-sac of bungalows. Each with its square lawn and boxed hedge. These were the gardens of those with the time for raising their own annuals and spraying roses. The blooms splattered colour along the edges of the grass, around doorways and windows.

The colt could run, he decided. Parnold's energy was not in doubt. There was a beauty in it. It was the love of being alive. Some found it in physical movement, others in mental activity, others in watching. Somehow police work combined all those ingredients for Campbell. "If only I could be left in peace by those efficiency experts to get on with it," he thought.

He took a lung-full of fenland air because even on the hottest day he knew there would always be movement in it.

Chapter 6

No, the face of the man she'd wanted all those years ago did not belong to the man she'd seen last night on the bridge. His age was wrong. Maggie rolled her head on her grey pillow. She fully realised her mistake now. It was not him. The features and shape of the body were similar. The man on the bridge had been older than she'd remembered him, perhaps heavier set, more how he might have looked in his fifties. He'd been twenty when she'd last seen him. He'd been older than her and all that happened took place sixty years since.

Had her dead father sent her this vision to rekindle all the misery of the past? He had hated her in life, so why not in death? Such a punishment seemed almost reasonable to her. Not one person could she risk loving now, but at seventeen she would have loved anybody. Her hunger for affection had been more than just her body cheating on her.

Only she'd remembered her sixteenth birthday that year, the year her father died.

Oh, how she remembered.

The ice was melting. She could hear the broken pieces clinking together in the River Sparrow. The water from the snow washed into the ditches and drains, but the pumps were still, unable to take the ice. Standing on the bridge Maggie saw the water close to the top of the riverbanks, and when she looked to the landward side she saw water running across the track from the base of the bank to the field. It formed a puddle, which grew wider as she watched.

The wireless that morning had given out the weather forecast. A storm was coming.

At lunchtime she'd seen men arriving on the banks. They'd shovelled clay along the top where the river and ice chipped away at the soil, and then pegged tarpaulins on top to protect the clay. They'd explained what they were doing when she'd taken them the lunch she'd made for them of pasties and bread.

'Why don't you get out of here, up to the air base?' a white haired man had asked as he'd eaten his food. 'All the villagers've gone, why hint you?'

She'd smiled and said nothing and gone home to make up the fire. Glowing hot ash had fallen on her father's slippers, but he hadn't moved. She'd squashed them out with fingertips wetted with her spit. She knew even the smell of burning slipper would not have woken him while alcohol was blended with his blood, but somehow she couldn't have let his feet burn. She'd nudged them away from the open stove and shut the door. It'd been nearly a shove.

He'd stirred and called her, 'Slut', then went back to sleep. The fire'd glowed up but a white chill had sent her knuckles blue.

From the bridge she watched the gang working the riverbank, forming a chain to pass on the materials. They had been working along the bank for hours and still they worked. She recognised one small dark-haired lad of her own age working next to his father. Beyond them, a fair head moved among the capped, hatted, grey and brown heads. All their hair was darkened by dampness, but his was still gleaming yellow as it turned and twisted above the others.

Having collected their tea from her kitchen she returned to the bank. This time she looked at the faces as she handed out the food. Some were deeply lined by a lifetime in the fenland wind, other faces were younger. The bodies of the older men were angular, squat, but they used an economy of movement the lithe smooth-faced men could not. She tried not to look too long at the blond man as she handed him his food. But he looked at her for longer than the others when he thanked her.

She realised how unused to people she was. All sorts of emotions and feelings soared up inside her. She didn't know what to do with them. She felt as raw and wild as the weather, which bit into her through her third-hand woollen coat. Suddenly, despite its largeness and length it seemed not to cover her body adequately. She wrapped it closer to herself.

The man next to the blond man told him to leave her alone. The dark blue eyes only left her to answer the man back. She heard his foreign accent. Her neck felt hot, she was cold. She must go home. She would make them more food. She would come again. Yes, that was what she'd do.

Back in her father's kitchen, flour was scattered over the table-top on the bath and over her forearms. Her skin was tight and tingling, it thrilled when she touched it. Her stomach and breasts screamed an urgency she didn't understand. She felt an urge to strip her clothes from her body, to be naked.

Because the scullery door was open Maggie saw her father lean over and drink from the bottle beside him. It was not worth hiding it from him, his anger was frightening. So let it kill him. She shut the door.

The lamps on the riverbank blinked at her as she splashed through the water bleeding through the base of the bank. It was escaping and so was she. With this thought she began to run towards the lanterns. She scrambled up the bank, hungry for a sight of the blond man.

The gale was blowing from the southwest. It pushed her across the bank towards the swollen river. She toiled along the bank bent double. They had worked themselves down to the bend some half-mile down river from the village. When she reached the gang of workmen they were up to their waists in water trying to plug a breach in the bank with sandbags. She was right up on them so she could hear their shouts. One man was yelling that the gales had taken down the telephone wires and he couldn't get through to the drainage board at Ely. Another man swore as his hurricane lamp blew out.

She saw the blond man. And he looked up. For a moment there was something in his dark blue eyes she didn't like, and then he smiled. His face changed. This second look of his went beyond her skin, her face, it went inside her. It was looking at her femaleness. It devoured it.

She weakened and the wind took her. The blond man passed his sandbag to the man next to him and caught hold of her. She allowed him to turn her in the direction of the lane.

'Where are you going, Jon?' yelled the man nearest them.

'Down the bank,' the blond man yelled back pointing at Maggie.

The man nodded. 'Come straight back,' he yelled.

Jon came further than the base of the bank. He walked along the lane through the seeping river water, past fields until they reached the pub. He paused. He looked around the empty village. She thought that he was thinking of turning back, but that was not the look in his eye. She didn't want him to go back to the riverbank. She wanted him to stay with her. She tugged at his sleeve and pointed out the entrance to the lane leading to the pump house. He smiled. She trembled.

She gladly fell against the pump house, when he pushed her against it. The yellow Victorian bricks felt hard against her back, and his body smelt strong against her. She felt soft, warm, damp and cold. And she wanted more. She slid from under him and went into the scullery and peeped through the living room door.

'Dare you?' asked Jon. Now she recognised his accent as German, so recently the enemy. She could feel him looking over her shoulder at her father.

'I dare do anything,' said Maggie.

Her father snored heavily as they crossed the living room to the near-ladder stairs. She glanced behind at him. He seemed old, older than the men on the bank, yet he was probably younger than many of them. His skin was grey and lined, his hair thin and white like a man of seventy, not long ago it had been thick and black. She knew he was just forty-five.

If only she'd known that face would haunt her...

Chapter 7

Campbell viewed the home of the seven listed vehicle numbers through the car windscreen. Vast metal buildings spanned one side of a yard with wide plastic strips hung across the doorways. Fork lift trucks moved in and out with their pallets of canned fen celery and carrots catching the strips. They pulled them over the top of the vehicles and moved on letting them fall into place behind. The concrete roadway was clean of litter and weeds. It was marked out with yellow paint, and signs indicated they should not travel faster than five miles an hour.

A temporary type of office building just beyond the entrance gates was marked "Reception", and Parnold was already making his initial enquiry inside.

'Main offices around the back,' said Parnold when he returned. 'There's a car park over there too.'

This office looked more comfortable, thought Campbell, leaving the car. Parnold had parked in one of the three spaces marked, "Visitor".

'Eira Dublin,' said Campbell, 'have you heard a name like that before?'

'A managing director too,' said Parnold.

Campbell paused by the door. 'I'll watch,' he said. The task of questioning someone with such a dubious name would suit Parnold, though Campbell would have to stop his colt before it ran into any barbed wire.

A woman in a flowing flower print frock showed them into the Managing Director's office, where a square man rose from his seat and became tall. He came round from behind his plain desk to greet them. Campbell guessed his age at about ten years his senior, mid-to-late fifties with his thinning, greying fair hair.

'Good day to you,' said Eira Dublin. 'Just the people I want to see.'

Campbell felt the man's handshake was firm and controlled while he nodded at the broad smile which invited them to take a seat. Southern Irish, Campbell noted.

'These numbers belong to your vehicles,' explained Parnold leaning slightly towards the Irishman now re-seated behind his desk.

'Do they now?' said Eira Dublin taking the list and examining it. 'Indeed they do. I reported the number plates stolen some time ago.'

'When?'

'About three months ago, must have been the end of February, beginning of March.'

Campbell liked the man's song filled voice. It seemed to embrace and love the air that it moved between.

'But I reported it. It must be on your records?' continued Eira Dublin.

What he said did tally with the information Campbell nursed in his notebook, but then why shouldn't it? If it were a lie, if he were really using his vehicles for illegal dumping, it would not be hard to be consistent.

'Several of my trucks were parked on a lorry park just on the outskirts of Ouse Crossing. The number plates were removed. I guessed they might go on stolen lorries, or ones being used to do something illegal, so I reported it immediately.'

'We will have to speak to the drivers,' said Parnold.

'Of course, I'll have my assistant look up their names.'

Campbell saw Eira Dublin's dark blue eyes catch the light coming through the vertical blinds at the window as he spoke to his secretary through an intercom.

'Do you have any connection with Sparrow Bank?' asked Parnold.

'This is about that car going into the river there last night, isn't it?' He didn't wait for a reply. 'I heard it on the news. I have a cottage there by that very bridge. It quite frightened me.'

Campbell wondered on what level this jovial man felt fear. He could see none of it on his face. His hands were beneath the desk, so he could not see if they were gripped or trembling, but somehow he doubted they were doing either.

'Were you at the cottage last night, Mr Dublin,' Parnold asked.

'No, I wasn't,' he replied. 'I fish and it's the closed season. And with the fruit starting we're very busy here. I've not had the cottage long anyway. I've stayed there twice so far, I should say.'

'What were you doing last night, Mr Dublin?' asked Parnold.

'I was having a rest at home with a book.'

'Were you alone?'

'I was babysitting the children. My wife went to see her mother. The old lady's been poorly.' Campbell noted the softness in Eira's voice.

'Can anyone confirm that for us?' asked Parnold.

'No, they can't,' said the Irishman. He smiled widely. 'And what ideas are you getting there now?'

'Why didn't you contact us about having that cottage by the bridge?' asked Parnold.

'I was going to tell you. I heard about the accident on the lunchtime news. But I haven't had the chance. Anyhow, I wasn't there so I hadn't seen anything. So what was there to say?'

Campbell saw the colour rising in Parnold's face. He knew the colt hadn't seen the barbed wire. It was time to draw in the reins.

'These are routine questions, Mr Dublin,' he said. 'At this stage we are keeping an open mind.'

The fact that he was the owner of the list of vehicle numbers found in Graham Pleasance's study and that he had a cottage next to the bridge where that same man died could be coincidence or circumstantial evidence. Campbell knew he couldn't be sure which they had, but he could see Parnold had made up his mind it was the later.

His thoughts were stopped by the secretary coming in with the list of drivers. Ideal, he would get Parnold to check them out tomorrow.

When Campbell thanked Eira Dublin, Parnold left the room. 'You're a long way from Ireland,' Campbell added conversationally. He hoped to get some of the man's history, but Eira replied with,

'And you from your home town, sir?' His smile was as bright as the late afternoon sun, thought Campbell.

'Aye,' he reluctantly agreed. Through the office door Parnold had left open Campbell could hear his Sergeant going down the stairs. He rose to leave, but the smartly dressed Managing Director slipped from his seat and closed the door.

'A moment before you go, Inspector. Let me show you a letter.'

Campbell read the offered sheet of white paper. It was headed with Kinera Kran's address and the words "code on can" followed by a list of numbers and letters.

"Dear Sir," he read,

"Last week I bought a can of your celery. (The label is enclosed.) I found this screw in it. A child could have choked on it. This has upset me greatly."

It was signed with a jerky line, which ended with a curl, and printed underneath was the name, "Mrs Kinera Kran".

Before he could comment Eira Dublin started talking, 'The screw doesn't fit any of our machinery. I accept that even though we have frequently checked the metal detectors an odd something might get through, but this is her fourth complaint, Inspector, about our products.'

'This is outside my area of investigation, Mr Dublin. I can pass this on. Has she tried to obtain money?'

'No, not exactly, but we always send a couple of tokens for our products. I feel her complaints are an insult to my integrity as a food producer. I don't want to see this woman prosecuted, after all she lives in the same village as my fishing cottage. But perhaps you could have a word with her?'

'We'll see,' said Campbell fingering the screw taped to the corner of the letter. He wondered if this might be useful, but he coughed and said, 'I am too busy for such petty nonsense, but I will pass it on to the right department.' So if he thought he could distract Campbell with this, it would be quite clear that he was mistaken.

'Thank you, Inspector.'

Back at the car Parnold had that look of "Where have you been?" Campbell ignored it and got out his notebook. He made two notes:

The letter from Kinera Kran could be a red herring to cover some connection Eira Dublin has with her – perhaps even his cottage?

Why didn't Dublin ask us what his lorry numbers had to do with the man drowning at Sparrow Bank? Was he too surprised to take it in or did he already know?

Nothing must be lost, he thought. He enjoyed the way details of the personalities had started to form little clusters of information in his mind. Those efficiency experts worrying themselves about numbers could not look inside his head, and counting, he was sure, would not catch criminals.

Campbell pulled at his seat belt. It jerked to a halt several times before he got it into its clip.

'His office,' said Parnold, his eyes fixed on the other traffic on the roundabout, 'might know about these registration numbers.'

Campbell knew he meant the workplace of Graham Pleasance (deceased) despite the fact that his name had not been mentioned for several minutes. He felt he was beginning to communicate with his young sergeant. Such a thing had never happened to him before. It surprised him that it gave him the sort of pleasure he associated with his family.

'It wouldn't hurt to cast our eyes over the victim's colleagues,' he agreed, thinking of the Chinese girl Graham Pleasance had been seen with the week before his death.

'His office is just across the way,' said Parnold. The car's indicator light was already flashing in the direction he was pointing out.

As Parnold swung the car into the parking area Campbell knocked his elbow against the window, and muttered, 'Slow down, can't you?' The feeling of easy understanding had gone, and he didn't regret it. Catching Parnold's amazed look, Campbell added, 'I was adjusting my seat belt.'

A bee buzzed at the open window while a high-speed fan flicked at papers under a paper weight of a dandelion clock embedded in glass. Campbell noted the captivity of a plant unable to shed its seeds, while flicking the bee out into the fresh air with a piece of paper. Partitions formed the rest of a square marking out the corner of the open plan office where Graham Pleasance would have sat.

'He didn't come in much,' said the girl who'd introduced herself as Katie and showed them this now unoccupied desk. 'We'll need it for his replacement.' Her pink and blue spectacles caught the sun from the window. She reached across the desk and pulled down a brown roller blind.

Parnold went through the desk. His fingers trotted through the papers, his neck and back arched in a display of his efficiency. Campbell wondered if it was for the benefit of this broad-hipped office junior.

'He spent a lot of time down at the lab,' she continued. 'He was involved with contaminated lands. Sometimes he would collect soil samples and take them down there. Part of his job was to list any land contaminated with toxic chemicals. It was a project he was doing for the Council.'

Campbell decided to just nod at this new information. "So Graham Pleasance was not only looking for dumpers, he was looking at old dump and factory sites for contamination," he thought. He remembered seeing some general pieces about it in the newspapers recently. Then he noticed Parnold was placing papers within easy reading distance. They were reports on various contaminated lands in the area. He asked Katie if she would make copies for them. She smiled and leaned against the desk making her short skirt ride up to her buttocks. Campbell could not avoid seeing her pale un-stockinged legs which seemed to him to be formed from clay instead of bone or muscle. They were smoothly shaped and translucent like porcelain, yet solid without veins or moles.

'It'll all have to be sorted anyway,' she said. 'They're advertising for Mr Pleasance's replacement next week,' and she wriggled her shoulders.

'And Mr Pleasance, what was he like?' asked Campbell.

'I don't miss him, if that's what you mean. He never said much when he was in, and that wasn't often, so I found him a bit boring. He did a lot of work outside normal office hours. I think he was dedicated to his work. But I'd never've guessed he'd come to that sort of an end.' With this Katie took the pile of papers to the photocopier.

When she came back she added, 'He wasn't what I would call a real man, if you know what I mean?' and she looked at Parnold, who smiled back.

Campbell decided that she only saw people through their sexuality and graded them accordingly. He wondered briefly how she would grade him, but couldn't give himself an answer.

'He did spend a lot of time down at the lab. The girl there could help you, I expect. Her name's Sheena Kiljames.' Katie unpinned a photo of an office Christmas party from the wall and pointed to a girl in the centre. 'She's Irish, believe it or not. Well, her parents were from Hong Kong or somewhere like that, anyway.' Then she added, 'But I told this to that policewoman that phoned about half an hour ago.'

'Ah,' said Campbell. 'Good.' The girl wasn't objecting to the duplication – she clearly enjoyed all the fuss.

In the picture Sheena's thick black hair was made into a single plait down her back. Her slender limbs were a rich coffee colour and her finger nails a soft unvarnished pink. A gold stud earring shone brightly against its dark background. Her neat nose and small, defined chin were in profile against a large red jumper worn by the bulky Graham Pleasance.

It had to be the girl seen with Graham Pleasance at Drain Farm and the Wet Goose pub. 'Can you find out an address for Sheena Kiljames?' asked Campbell.

'I can phone the lab, if you wait a minute,' said Katie winking through her spectacles.

Ten minutes later Campbell split the pile of papers in half and put Sheena Kiljames's home address in his notebook.

'She's on holiday, but she didn't tell anyone that she was going away, so you might find her at home,' informed Katie.

Campbell passed one, slightly larger, pile to Parnold and picked the other one up himself. All this data ought to be entered on the computer but he wanted to go through it. 'These papers are surprisingly heavy,' he said, but he felt a good deal of progress had been made for a first day, so he smiled and patted them. 'Grand weather,' he added. By the time they reached the car Campbell had decided that they must check on Sheena Kiljames before calling it a day, and said so to Parnold.

Chapter 8

Maggie remembered waking in her father's bed that night, the night of the storm. It was her bed now. The patchwork quilt was her mother's work. It had been newer then. It had curved over their bodies…

She wondered how long she'd slept here naked and in the dark next to him. How long had it been since she'd taken food to the gang working on the riverbank? And the man downstairs, her father, had he heard them? And the man next to her… No, she wouldn't ask him his past -- or ask him to stay. Such a thing would be impossible with her father here.

She wanted to touch the man in her bed, feel his skin, let his blond hair tickle her fingers. She reached out.

A noise too small for her to work out caught her. Instead of touching Jon she went to the door. Was her father waiting on the other side? The door latch clunked as she lifted it. Standing on the triangle of wood that formed the landing she peered down into the living room. At first she couldn't make out anything except the light coming from the open range. It was barely a glow. Then there was a movement.

'Father?' Her voice shook on its way out of her. There was no reply, so she went back to the bedroom for the lamp. Still the man in the bed slept. The noise was louder now. Scratching, that's what it was. She was sure.

Having burnt her fingers from lighting the lamp she took it to the landing. An arc of light caught the rough brick floor and a dark movement across it. She could see a mass of small bodies moving about the room, milling and turning, scrabbling at cupboards. From here she could only part of her father she could see was his slippers. A rat pushed past them. There were no rats living in her home. Where could so many of these creatures have come from?

A piercing noise came from her; she hadn't wanted to scream.

The man she'd been touching was next to her snatching the lamp from her. She didn't want to disagree with him. More than that, she wanted to give him her whole self, even her free will.

'You'll drop it,' he was saying. 'The whole place will catch fire.' Then, 'Come away.'

Part of her wanted to. His body was an escape. She let him pull her back into the bedroom until she heard some other part of herself say that she had to help her father and between them they could get him upstairs.

'Don't you see?' she said putting on her shirt and skirt. Covering herself made it easier for her to withdraw from him. She knew now why the rats were here. 'The river is going to flood. The rats are trying to escape. We must bring him up.' Couldn't this man with this lustful body think?

He nodded, put on his shirt and trousers and followed her down. She told him to shut the door behind him as she kicked a rat out of her way.

When she reached the bottom of the stairs she ran to the scullery and fetched a broom. She screamed and yelled and chased them out of the room her father still slept in. She'd opened the door to the yard, fetched the broom, and herded them through, back to the field. Before she shut the back door on them she glanced up at the riverbank. This was not a weak point, she knew that. The bank would give way up by the bend. They would probably be safe upstairs. She took the timberwork top off the bath and jammed it against the door to fill the gap underneath where the rats had got in. She placed the iron and some cooking pans against it, followed by a brace made with the broom. Then she went back to the living room.

Jon was swigging at her father's bottle.

'Can you take his arms?' she asked. He did as he was asked, and she took the slumbering man's legs. The weight pulled at her back. To look at him, with his muscles wasted by alcohol, you would not think he could be so heavy, thought Maggie. She lost her grip on one of his legs. It slithered away and dropped its slipper. 'Wait,' she called and gathered it up. Inside she accused him of not wanting to be saved.

Jon kicked a remaining rat off the stair he was on. It caught Maggie across her naked ankle. On the landing Jon opened the door to her little bedroom. The bed was as neat as she'd left it that morning. Her father had made no sound, only breathed, throughout his rescue and now, as they laid him on the bed, he groaned. She hated him. He wouldn't thank her for saving his life.

'Suppose this house is washed away?' she asked her lover. His answer was to take her back to her father's bed. She shut her bedroom door behind them leaving her father in her room to sleep. Then, once inside, she shut the door closing herslf and her lover in her father's bedroom. She felt safer now as if the door could shut out all the risks and fears of a life outside this room. Jon was already pulling at her shirt, and she wanted him to.

Looking through the gap in her bedroom curtains Maggie saw Kinera Kran painting in her studio.

'Pretty pictures,' she said holding a torn and mended photograph in her pocket. It used to stand on the drawers, she remembered, until she had broken the frame the day her little cousin, Janet, had seen it. She'd smashed it against the wall. "No one must ever see the evil we made together," she thought.

She rubbed her thumb over its surface. It was worn to a soft felt. He had been hers for a short while, and this was all she had left of him now.

'Father, forgive me. Don't send me any more ghosts,' she said. 'I was sixteen years old. I wanted a lover. I needed to be wanted. I thought he would be with me always. What did you give me? Only misery. And you said I weren't your child. I've been punished enough.' The lament caressed her.

She must have brushed the curtains because Kinera Kran looked up. Maggie moved away, yellow tears running down her face. She called to her cats. She would feed them. It would soon be dark, and then they would walk the riverbanks together.

The blackness of the sky, the stars, the full moon rising like a new sun over the fens – this was the sort of night Maggie lived for. Even if the bridge looked alien with its little orange lights flashing on and off at different times, she was going to enjoy her prowl.

When she ran up the bank two cats scampered by as if they were racing with her. She laughed and threw a stone into long grass for a third cat to chase. This was her only freedom and that watchful Kran woman would not take it from her. She turned and walked along the bank looking at that woman's house without meaning to. She could sort her out, she didn't know how just yet, but she was sure she could.

Then she stopped. She'd been walking away from the village. Her view of the bridge was perfect. There was someone walking over it from her side to Kran's side – north to south. The form broke across some of the orange lights. From this distance she couldn't even see if it was a man or a woman.

Maggie shuffled along the bank until she was nearly back at her cottage and crouched in the grass. She hadn't lost sight of the person on the bridge. The woman – she was sure of that now, by the way she moved – climbed over the handrail and jumped down onto the riverbank that ran opposite Maggie.

It was the sort of night for a riverside ramble. But walking on the road would be easier, surely. This woman was almost scrambling along the bank. No one would walk back to their house like that. It had to be the Kran woman or her friend – just because they lived together didn't mean they didn't have secrets from each other. Everyone had secrets. She knew that. Her own secret being the most dreadful one she thought could exist. These were silly women, as far as she could see, inventing troubles for themselves where probably none really existed.

Yes, she could see it was Kinera Kran. The woman crept over the bank next to her house. 'Now we shall see,' said Maggie. 'Your evil little notes through my door will be your undoing. Call me a snooper, would you? Now I shall be just that.'

A light coming on inside the studio window made her look up. She could see Kinera, with a cigarette in her hand, coming across the room to look out.

Maggie wouldn't knock on the door but she would wait and face her on the riverbank. Fight against the lies Kinera twisted about her. She would wait by the door. This would be a real cat's game. She smiled to herself and set off back along the bank to cross the river.

But once on the bridge she could not smile. It would never be the same again. The lights, the plastic tape, the hole – they all frightened her. And when she stood where HE had stood last night she could not bear to be on the bridge any longer. She turned her head towards the river and felt along the railing opposite the gap until she reached the road on the other side.

Her favourite cat mewed at her. 'Go home,' she said but she didn't mean it.

She walked along the top of the bank. The grass was thicker down where Kinera'd walked earlier. But very few people had come along here since the end of the fishing season and the slope was too steep for cattle. She dropped down to the lane side of the bank before the light cast across the river from Kinera's studio would give her away. With the moon behind the house the rest of the building cast a shadow across the lower half of the bank. Maggie knew that here she would not easily be seen from the front door or Kinera's studio window. The air was warm and still here. She could wait and watch for hours and no one need know. Pushing her legs out in front of her Maggie let herself sit down. About an hour later she leaned back on the grass. The studio light spanned the top of the bank, but it was still the only light on in the building. The cat nudged itself onto Maggie's lap. She kissed it.

How could she have closed her eyes? She never slept at night. That was when the ghosts came to haunt her. And she had to wake herself now and properly. Maggie could feel someone over her, watching. Whoever it was, whatever it was, touched her. She opened her eyes and jumped up in one movement, keeping her cat clutched to her. Looking up she thought she saw the face she'd seen last night lit by the pub's security light. But this time the light was behind him casting his features in shadow. He was holding her shoulder.

She pulled away and ran. Without stopping she soon reached the bridge and then the bank near her old wind-pump home, and, a moment after that, her own back door.

Inside, the cat clawed away from her and she tried to think clearly about what she'd seen. Had it been a ghost or a human? Had it been smiling or sneering? She couldn't tell. He was the same build as the man on the bridge, and that of her lover from over fifty years ago. The face was like theirs too.

No, no, no, she would not remember any more of her past. She did not want to. She refused. And yet there was her father's face. This time beneath the dirty washing-up water she'd left in the sink. It broke the surface and called, 'Help me.'

She went to the scullery door. For a moment it wouldn't open. When she got through it she slammed it shut behind her and made for the stairs. Scrambling up them she slipped on the top one and knelt there crying.

'I can't run away from you because you're inside my head,' she said angrily. 'I know you are.' To prove this to herself she looked down the stairs. Her father's face was there floating under soil covered water instead of the reality of her living room. The face slithered to the top and called, 'Help me.'

'It's all too late. You don't know how it was.' She had to tell him what happened: the truth, once and for always. She found herself whispering. She could hardly dare to say the words.

Her muscles must be made of milk, Maggie thought, lying in the bed, her body touching Jon's, one leg caught between his. The water had arrived down stairs. They'd crept out on the landing to look. It had been dark and smelly so they'd giggled and returned to her father's bed, while her father slept in hers. That thought made her giggle some more.

This time when she woke with a pleasant weakness and a compliance in her body she found herself trying to fight these sensations. Because, this time there was a noise. Not the rats, it was clearer than that. Yes, she was sure now. It was a human voice.

Stumbling from the bed she dragged her old coat around her and made for the door in the dull light cast by the oil lamp on the chest of drawers.

The freezing floodwater chilled the air. It lapped three steps down, but the landing was wet. Her feet slipped. She caught the edge of the door to stop herself sliding into the flood. Then she heard the sound again. A man calling for help.

'Dad, is that you?' she called. Her only reply came from her father's bed:

'What's going on?' said Jon. 'Come back here.'

'I heard Father shout for help. I know I did.'

'Check the other bedroom. He probably shouted out in his sleep.'

The other door on the landing was shut. She opened it. The room was dark. She had to go in to see if the man she'd left on the bed was still there. Her hands and arms felt along the bedcover. It was crinkled, warm and empty.

The shout came again, choked and shrill.

'The drunken fool's fell in,' she groaned.

There were two strides between her little bed and the landing. She took them and stepped down the ladder-like stairs until her chin was level with the freezing water. Then she saw him holding a hook in the ceiling of the living room.

'Jon, I can't reach him. Please help me. I can't reach him. I can't swim.'

'Nor can I,' said Jon now standing above her on the landing. 'We can't help him. Leave him.'

'I can't.'

'Who do you want?'

She knew what he meant. Wouldn't any man leave her if her father were to survive? She didn't want him to go. Yet, 'He's drowning,' she said.

Jon yanked her arm off the top step and pushed her backwards into the water. 'You can go and get him,' he said. The cold water chilled her legs and cramped her stomach.

'I can't. I can't swim.'

'Then come with me.'

She was hauled up the steps sobbing. On the landing she called over her shoulder, 'Dad hang on. I'll get help.' Her body buckled under her as cramps screwed her muscles. She gasped as she clutched her legs to her stomach.

'There is no help and you know it. What a cruel thing to say to a drowning man,' he said.

'What about those men from the riverbank?

'They won't be there. They'll be long gone.' His voice was hard.

'You don't know.' Maggie scrambled on her hands and knees for the bedroom window. But she didn't get there. Her coat was wrenched from her. 'He's dying,' she sobbed. Her body lurched as tears caught in her throat. And she closed her eyes. She didn't want this man inside her again, but there was no escape. She pulled away from him but found herself trapped against the wall. He placed his hands about her throat, a threat. She screamed, but it was too late. She felt tight and alone.

And afterwards she was sore and bruised. She wanted to wash his scent from her, but the only water was the filthy cold floodwater.

Jon taunted her by saying she enjoyed her lover while her father drowned.

He slept across the bed while Maggie went back to the landing and shouted to her father. There was no answer for a moment. Then she heard a knocking sound, a soft thud against the ceiling below her. She lowered herself into the cold dark water and reached out. She knew when she touched it what it was. Her whole being wanted him to be alive even though the flesh and clothing in her hand was cold and unmoving.

When she pulled her father towards her his face looked like a mask it was so pale. His eyes were open as if he could see her from some other existence. But these were dead eyes, accusing eyes. She did not scream.

Maggie wiped her eyes on her pink cardigan. She never understood where she'd got the strength to get her father back into her own little bedroom. She'd tried to get him on the bed, but had given up. Then the boat had come. Men had shouted and tapped at the bedroom windows. For a moment she'd wondered why they were there, who had they come to rescue? It was all too late.

In a matter of minutes she and Jon had been with them. They had no room on the boat for her father's body, but there was another boat coming up behind, they'd said.

'I did my best. I didn't know what to do,' said Maggie to her father's ghostly image as it sunk out of sight in her imagined floodwaters. But she had realised too late that she could have done more to save him. Hadn't she been fulfilling her lustful body when he'd died? That was the way her father would have seen it and how Jon had said it had been.

Couldn't she have tied blankets together and thrown him a lifeline, or broken the frame of one of the beds to make a pole?

'I'm sorry. I'm so sorry. Please, no more ghosts, Father. I cannot bear them and why are they versions of Jon. They are not the right age. He would be old now and he was so much younger then. It makes no sense…' And she stopped. She was aware of a memory she'd buried deep because it was so painful it rent her apart. It bubbled up like air from drowning lungs to take her to the brink of insanity. She realised the guilt she'd carried over the death of her father had only been a mask for her greater crime. Since her seventeenth birthday it had lain hidden from her.

She allowed herself to slither down the steps. She wished death upon herself and smashed her head against the floor.

'Matthew. My son. This is the ghost you have sent me, Father. He would be about the right age. Kill me now. Have your ghost of Matthew kill me. Yes, I should have died when he did, Father. You are right.'

Chapter 9

Campbell was feeling irritable as he sat in the car park just outside Bishop's Town. The water in the disused sand quarries reflected the blue of the sky. People walked through the wooded slope in front of him. Dogs sniffed each other and the ground. Campbell had turned sideways so that his legs could feel the sun while he looked through the papers from Graham Pleasance's desk. It wasn't the having to look through these documents which was annoying him, he told himself, it was the frustration of not getting hold of that Sheena Kiljames girl.

And Jenner had wittered on about being sent to do a job and then he'd covered the same ground himself. He'd tried Sheena's home at Ouse Crossing last night and again this morning. At least today there'd been a neighbour getting in her milk off the doorstep and she'd told him that Sheena was on holiday, but Sheena hadn't told anyone where she was going. The tightly curled grey head of the neighbour had nodded. 'Dark horse that one,' she'd said.

He'd tried other neighbours but no one had known where she was.

He turned another page of Graham Pleasance's papers while one part of his mind gnawed at the morning's events. He'd dispatched Parnold to talk to Eira Dublin's drivers with the number plates from the list from Graham Pleasance's study at home. Meanwhile, Campbell had gone down to Drain Farm.

This trip to the place where Sheena Kiljames and Graham Pleasance had been seen had been slightly more useful, he supposed. The farmer had been there and he'd told him that, 'This couple from the Council' were surveying his land because it had been used in the last war by the Ministry, and that was all he knew.

He turned some more pages on his lap and mulled over the fact that a large woman delivering post on a bicycle had interrupted his conversation with the farmer.

He'd recognised her as Janet Sparrow. Even though she must've been nearly the same age as himself he'd felt that she looked much older. Her yellow hair was nearly grey and the fen winds had worried her skin into lines, which marked laughter and sorrow equally. She'd rattled on about how her Auntie Maggie's mother had been killed in what was now the daffodil field down the road during the war. A British aeroplane had crashed there shortly after taking off from a nearby airfield. And before Janet had finished her story the farmer had gone.

But Janet Sparrow's earlier information about Graham Pleasance and Sheena Kiljames being at Drain Farm had been useful. After all, that was why he'd gone down there.

With that thought he flipped through some more papers on his lap. But he just could not keep his mind on them.

Yet surely the farmer was a suspect, he thought. If his land was contaminated he would have wanted Graham Pleasance and Sheena Kiljames killed before the samples were taken. Afterwards would be too late, but here among Graham's office papers was a copy of the laboratory form. There was a squiggle across it saying it had been received by the lab.

He picked up his radio to make a telephone link. A receptionist at the public analyst's laboratory put him through to one of Sheena Kiljames' colleagues.

'We received those samples through the post,' the girl confirmed.

'Do you know where Sheena Kiljames has taken her holiday?' he asked hoping she might be a friend of hers. Jenner had had no luck with her enquiries on the subject.

'No, I'm afraid Sheena keeps herself very much to herself,' was the reply. So, yet again, he went back to his pile of papers -- once he'd made a note in his notebook to check whether the farmer knew that the samples had gone in. Among this heap of documents there must be plenty of contaminated lands, he decided. The farmer might not be the only person with that motive.

He looked up as a young couple walked by calling their dog away from the pit and remembered his nightmare from last night. He liked his dreams to sort his thoughts, but this one sorted nothing. It started with a tidal wave coming towards him in his car. Kinera Kran, Mrs Sturning and Bonita

Arlotte were passengers. The water didn't roar, it seeped into the car and none of them moved or said anything. He recalled looking upwards at the surface of the water above him and not being frightened. Then he'd woken up.

Here it was. The paper now on top of the pile was the list of potentially contaminated lands Graham Pleasance was working to. He held it up. 'Yet Graham's successor is bound to use the same list – so only short-sighted murderers need apply.' He was about to give up on the idea of kissing the list when he felt a twinge of cramp in his leg. He bent down to rub it and stopped to look at the document on his lap, which had been underneath the one, he was now holding.

'There's a familiar name here, Kran, not Kinera, but Kenneth. That's what the Spanish girl said her patron's husband was called,' he said. And, he noted the man's address, which was the only writing on the page, down in his notebook. Didn't Kinera say her husband introduced her to Graham Pleasance at the seaside? This was interesting, but he was still worried about Sheena Kiljames so he lifted the radio to contact the office. They would have to find her, put a call out for her on the media.

When he'd spoken to the press liaison officer, the voice on the radio told him the Chief wanted to see him in his office, now.

Campbell approached Kenneth Kran's office. This was a rectangular grey temporary-type surrounded by yellow diggers and lorries, situated halfway between Sparrow bank and Hillvill. Any Pleasure he might have had at chasing this lead had been much reduced by his visit to the Chief's office. The result was the man next to him in the passenger seat. His full beard and glasses were still, only his pen moved over the sheet of paper on his clipboard making ticks in boxes every three minutes. Just him being there was enough to prevent Campbell thinking straight.

He shook his head and got out of the car, happy to leave the time-use-study man behind. But before he got to the office door the small man was at his shoulder. He looked almost as if he was in a bad disguise, thought Campbell. He rolled backwards on his heels.

'What was your name again?' he asked the efficiency consultant.

'Alec Gowan.' This, Campbell noted was said with his mouth only, and that barely moved. Was it economy, or an attempt to look completely neutral, or was it simply a lack of character, he wondered.

The bell was answered. For a moment Campbell thought by some magic the owner of the food factory, Eira Dublin, was about to open the dimpled glass screen. The broad outline and pale hair made familiar shapes until the screen slid sideways. Then he saw that this man was shorter and heavier in build and features. His face was tanned and rough unlike Dublin's almost white smooth skin. But his eyes were a similar dark blue.

'Yes?' asked the man. His voice was deep and rasping.

'Kenneth Kran?'

'Who wants to know?' The accent was clipped. The public school English sounded as if it was being spat out.

'Inspector Campbell, Police.' Campbell displayed his identity card. He noticed him looking past him at Alec Gowan.

'What's he doing?' he asked.

'Alec Gowan is involved in a time use study,' said Campbell without apology.

'Christ, they really know how to waste tax payers' money. Come in. I'm Kran.'

Their movement into the small office meant Campbell avoided having to agree with him. When they were arranged about Kenneth Kran's desk he asked him if he had known Graham Pleasance.

'Yes, I did,' said Kenneth Kran. 'I'm not surprised though. Graham Pleasance was a bit of a law unto himself. He used to say things to me which he had no right to say. Mind you, I never lodged a complaint. My business is built around the waste trade, Inspector. I get rid of stuff nobody wants. I'm a licensed operator.'

'What sort of things did he say?'

'He would swear and rant,' said Kenneth Kran. 'He had the manners of a cur. A lot of it dates back a couple of years, when he first started. I was buying tickets for dumping rubbish up at the tip from men working on the highways. They were digging soil, rock, old tarmac, that sort of thing from roadwork operations. And instead of dumping it up the tip they were dumping it on the roadside, waste ground, anywhere they could and letting me have the tip tickets cheaper than I could buy them through official sources. It was all harmless enough.'

'And?' asked Campbell, pulling out the word with his Edinburgh accent.

'Graham Pleasance put a stop to it. He introduced special tip passes for the highways lot and tightened up on the contractors running the tip. End of story. I took it as the end of a nice little number, but he labelled me a villain.' Kenneth Kran stretched out and twizzled on his office chair then glared at Alec Gowan, who was still ticking his boxes. Kran looked pleased with himself so Campbell asked him where he was last night.

'Oddly enough I was at Sparrow Bank.'

'Were you with anyone?'

'Yes, Bonita Arlotte. She's a friend of my wife's. She lives with her at Sparrow Bank. You shouldn't be asking me what happened. I saw nothing. You want to be asking his Chinese girl.'

'Oh?' asked Campbell meaning, "What do you know about Sheena Kiljames?"

'I know they were at it. You can tell these things, Inspector. They were always touching each other.'

'Can Bonita Arlotte vouch for your movements last night?'

'Yes, she can,' he smirked. "Till the rumpus started about the car in the river. Then I left.'

'What time would that have been?'

'I really don't know, Inspector. It was a while after we heard the splash but before you lot turned up. Now I'm extremely busy. If you've finished, you can take your little scribe away with you.'

Campbell noted the reddening of his neck and made a comment about the hot weather and left.

A short distance from Kenneth Kran's yard Campbell lurched the car across the road and stopped in a lay-bye. He wanted to digest the interview he had just had. He realised Alec Gowan thought differently when he said, 'I'm entitled to a break now.' His glasses twitched on his nose. It was nearly emotion, thought Campbell, but not quite.

'That's as maybe, but I'm not stopping for you,' said Campbell. He got out of the car shut the door and opened his notebook. He wrote, "Kenneth Kran is not telling me something and he is capable of dishonesty. Is he capable of murder? Not for something that happened two years ago anyway." He reached through the car window and dropped his notebook on the driver's seat and took his sandwiches from a cold bag in the boot of the car. He started eating.

Alec Gowan said, 'I thought you weren't taking a break.'

'I changed my mind,' replied Campbell, making sure it sounded like, "I do what I want when I want." 'Free minds solve cases, not those cluttered up with tick boxes,' he added. He watched Alec Gowan unwrap a pack of hot sandwiches that had spent the morning in the front parcel tray. They appeared limp and sweaty.

Parnold was sure Eira Dublin's drivers knew nothing. Each of his questions had been answered with a 'Yes' or a 'No' or a blank stare. He watched them leaving in their lorries, through his car windscreen and pulled the stopper out the end of his ballpoint pen with his teeth. He squeezed the plastic so that it suckered on to the end of his tongue.

Policing had always seemed more colourful with Graham Pleasance, more urgent, more exciting. All Campbell did was let him make an infinite number of enquiries which were totally unrelated to the crime, as far as he could see. Campbell was tying up police men and women on pointless exercises whereas Graham Pleasance had always got to the nub of the problem.

Eira Dublin's secretary walked across the factory yard towards the offices. Parnold saw her pat down her floral frock, which curved over her full breasts and her gently rounded, pregnant stomach. Her wedding ring caught the sun and he marvelled for a moment at the pleasure of human fertility. And, briefly, he wondered what it would feel like to be a father.

'I wonder if Mr Sturning's about,' said WDC Jenner. She made herself stand firmly on the worn red carpet of the Wet Goose saloon bar. Every muscle ached, but she was determined not to push at the strand of fair hair that had escaped from its pleat on the back of her head. She looked at WPC Garden next to her. Her fuzzy brown ponytail was damp where it touched her neck. They were both tired. Questioning the villagers had taken longer than she'd thought.

She and Garden had been given this side of the river to question, leaving out Mrs Maggie Norrice at the old wind-pump cottage as Campbell and Parnold had already tried her as well as Mrs Elizabeth Sturning at the pub. There was by far the largest number of houses on this side of the river and any of them could have heard or seen was a car roaring down the road. It had been this that had woken many of the villagers. At least she and Garden didn't have to see that Kran woman and her sidekick. She'd heard enough about them from Parnold, especially the Spanish girl.

WPC Garden was easing her bottom onto a barstool, and Jenner'd just raised an eyebrow at her when she heard grunts and shuffles coming from a room beyond the bar.

'Just moving a barrel. Be with you in a minute,' called a gruff London accent. He came through the door. He filled it widthways. With his ruddy face and the pink rims around his brown eyes Jenner knew that alcohol was more than just his job.

'Can I pour you a drink?' His steely slick-backed hair sat solidly on his head when he nodded at them. Jenner placed his age at over sixty.

She quickly declined the offer; Garden's answer was slower.

'Mind you, I don't know why I'm bothering to be polite to you lot. We had another break-in last night.'

'Did you report it?' asked Jenner.

'No what's the point? There was nothing nicked this time.'

Jenner wanted to move on so she explained, 'You weren't in when Inspector Campbell called by and spoke to your wife, Mr Sturning.'

'You're quite right there, love.'

'Who was in the bar the night before last, Mr Sturning?'

'Ooh very formal!' mocked Sturning.

'Pack it in, Harry,' complained a woman standing up from behind the bar with a scrubbing brush in her hand. She was considerably younger than Harry. Jenner thought it quite remarkable how close a match the brush was to the woman's hair. 'Don't listen to him he's daft,' Mrs Sturning continued. 'I was in the kitchen doing the cooking so I didn't see nothing, but we was busy that night – for a week-day, anyhow.'

Jenner winced, Mrs Sturning's voice was shrill. 'Who was in the bar the night the car went in the river?' she repeated.

'Funny you should ask that, love,' conceded Mr Sturning.

Jenner's initial amusement at these Punch and Judy characters was wearing thin. Her pen twitched.

'Now don't get impatient, love,' said Sturning.

'Could you just answer the question, Mr Sturning,' said Garden from her perch on the barstool.

'Course, Honey-bunch, anything you say.' He beamed at her. Jenner was disgusted to see her colleague blush under her fluffy fringe. He beamed at them both and continued, 'There was a few of the villagers in – mostly nice old boys, playing dommies in a corner. Dominoes to you, love. And then there were the others – that Spanish bit for one. She was with a man. At first I thought it was the Irishman.'

'Irishman?' asked Jenner.

'Yes. He's just bought a cottage in the village. He's a tall blond chap. "Dublin," I says, "Good to see you." He turns round, and it ain't him – he's shorter, less good looking. I hadn't seen him before.' His dark eyes challenged her.

'And the "Spanish Bit"?' queried Garden, who, Jenner remembered, hadn't already heard about her from Parnold.

'Bonita Arlotte,' he said. His pink eyeballs grew wide as if he could see her again standing by the window.

'I reckon,' said Mrs Sturning, 'that there are face families. You go on holiday and see people that look like folk back home, but they're not them. And you know when someone dies how you think you see them in the street, but it always turns out to be someone else. I did that when my dear old dad passed on.' She was interrupted by a dog's howl coming through from the yard. Mrs Sturning said, 'What's wrong with that dog now?' and left.

'And there were two women. One had been in here in the week, a Chinese girl. She'd been with that man that drowned, Graham Pleasance. He wasn't with her, mind. She was with this girl I hadn't seen before, a tall lanky thing. They were talking together in a corner, but they didn't stop long. They looked a bit heated but I couldn't hear what they were saying.'

'Thank you, Mr Sturning,' said Jenner, writing this last detail down.

'And we didn't see nothing the night before last, girlies. I would have told that Scotch git if he'd seen me. Pardon me French.' He said the last three words as if to say, "I couldn't care less what I say."

Out in the hot sun Jenner contacted Campbell. The car metal was hot. Garden jumped at the static shock she got from the door handle. Jenner smiled. Garden looked offended.

'I could've smashed his face in,' said Jenner. 'All those "loves", "girlies" and even a "honey-bunch". And you have to blush.'

Garden took off her shoes while she replied, 'At least he had something to tell us, which is more than you can say for most of them this morning.'

'Campbell and Parnold are on their way back to the village,' said Jenner after a brief conversation into the radio. 'We'll give the boss this information when he gets here.' She put back the hand set, slid into the passenger seat and pulled off her shoes.

Once she'd scrambled up the bank the bird sanctuary spread out before Sheena Kiljames. Patches of sky coloured water mixed with the green of rushes and grass covered the land as far as the eye could see. The flatness was broken by small trees, hedgerows, fences and summer grazing cattle. She laid her sickle on the grass and turned down her waders. She decided her waterproof jacket made a dry enough seat so she got out her sandwich box and ate her tea.

She couldn't work out why today's solitude did not have its usual pleasure. She wanted it to soften her shoulders and lighten her body as it usually did, but it wouldn't, not today. She always made herself forget about work when she was on holiday. She wouldn't even listen to the radio.

'Graham Pleasance is doing this to me,' she said out loud. He was more than just work. Her natural energy had turned into a kind of madness with him. The other night she'd told his stupid daughter what she'd thought of her and gone back to the campsite she'd pitched on the weekend before. She would have to untangle herself from his obsession.

Was it her imagination or had the birds moved away? Why had the cattle's grazing taken them into another pasture? She felt deserted.

Even the observatory didn't seem to have its usual role of kindly guardian. It seemed to spy on her. So she moved her coat and food over to the windbreak of willow to hide from any unseen eyes. She knew how powerful a watcher could be armed with lenses and cameras. For a moment she was one of the birds, but she knew about the watchers and they did not.

In the distance she heard a tractor being started up. The sound weakened as it moved away. Sheena screwed her cup back onto the flask and picked up her sickle.

She wondered if her mixed blood gave her these confusions of insight. An Irish father and her mother from Hong Kong she knew to be an unusual mix, but she was beginning to realise just how much she liked to blame her problems on her parenthood.

The sun was too hot. Surely this weather would bring thunderstorms soon. 'Ah well,' she sighed. She left her belongings where they were and headed for the dyke she'd been clearing. The ground was too soft and the habitat too precious for the job to be done mechanically. Her face softened at the task before her. She would enjoy cutting the choking growth away from the water. She would do it until blisters formed on her hands and her back ached. For her this would be wonderful. The water around her knees would again see sunlight.

The reeds moved. She looked up to see which of nature's creatures she might have disturbed. She half-turned, but she only caught a glimpse of a shoulder and arm clad in a green wax coat similar to her own, before being propelled towards the water. She felt it rush up her nose and pour into her ears. Her scream was being drowned. She lashed out behind her with her sickle. It was catching something until it was wrenched from her hand.

Surely she could live. Her heart, her brain, her body didn't want to give up. An extra small heart seemed to be throbbing in her throat. She choked on it.

She knew she took in her last breath as she filled her lungs with water.

Chapter 10

Campbell watched the clouds above the row of poplar trees while Parnold drove. He tried to ignore the presence of Alec Gowan with his clipboard and endless ticking pen.

The cloud shapes were defined by the blue sky behind them forming monstrous cumulus animals. An American bomber screamed under them on its way to the coast.

In contrast, they were heading towards Sparrow Bank from the south. The road was only wide enough to take the police car. Campbell nodded his thanks to a group of strawberry pickers standing in one of the pull off areas that were positioned along one side of the road to allow traffic to pass.

The night of Graham Pleasance's murder just one car had been heard roaring away down this straight road. Campbell noted the roughness of the surface which, he guessed, was from an earlier wartime concrete construction. The police car was not travelling quickly yet he could feel every bump and hole.

Along the opposite side to the passing place ran a drain twice the width of the road. Its lip was level with the road surface with reeds making a cream fringe above. The water level was a man's height below the edge of the drain, and Campbell could just see the heads of swans moving about on its surface.

The car swung across a flat, side-less, concreted bridge over to Drain Farm. Behind the farm buildings an open sided wooden and canvas structure had been put up in a nearby field. It seemed to Campbell that the population of a village was there walking or crouching among the strips of yellow straw and dark green strawberry plants. Coloured scarves were wrapped around women's hair while bowed men wore tattered hats. The tanned arms moving along the rows seemed as if they were pulling the bodies of the pickers along behind like so much unnecessary baggage.

The farmer hitched his belt up under the overhang of his belly as Parnold went to speak to him. Campbell only wanted it confirmed that him having potentially contaminated land was not a motive for murdering Graham Pleasance, and Parnold could do that. He smiled slightly to see Alec Gowan follow his sergeant. He would go in a different direction.

The air this afternoon was even hotter than it had been yesterday. The weather would change soon. It had to, thought Campbell. Casting his eye over the strawberry fields he saw two figures seated on canvas chairs at its edge. He recognised them. It was Bonita Arlotte and Kinera Kran sketching and painting. Bonita was involved in drawing the line of pickers close by. Kinera was producing a watercolour of a strawberry plant in between taking sips from a red plastic beaker standing on the ground next to her.

'Very good,' said Campbell using his Edinburgh accent to give the words authority.

'Thank you,' said Bonita sounding equally Spanish.

'These are only sketches, Inspector,' said Kinera. 'I will use them to make a much more dramatic picture than the pretty representation of a strawberry field.'

Campbell breathed in the sweet scent of strawberries. He felt the sun reflected off the straw and, as he looked along the rows, distant pickers shimmered in the heat haze.

'I went to see your husband, Mrs Kran,' he said. 'He's in the waste trade.'

'You could say that,' said Kinera washing her brush and laying it down in her wooden paint box. 'He's a complete waste, Inspector.'

'Have you seen him recently?'

'Do you think he murdered Graham Pleasance?' she countered.

'I can't rule anybody out at this stage, Mrs Kran.'

'He's a murderer, Inspector. You arrest him,' she said.

'What do you mean by that?'

He saw Kinera shake herself slightly and refocus her eyes on her painting. 'He's a devious crook, that's all. I can't give him an alibi for the night of the murder if that's what you want. But he did come to see me last night.'

'You said he was a murderer.'

'That was me just being a vicious divorcee, Inspector. Do you always listen to malice?' The slight turn of her shoulder told him she would say no more. He turned to look at the covered weighing area where Parnold, shadowed by Alec Gowan, was speaking to the farmer. He could see Parnold standing stiffly under the gaze of the efficiency expert.

'I'll walk back with you,' said Bonita, tossing a strand of her long black hair away from her face. Campbell nodded and started to pick his way along the edge of the field. This was what he'd hoped for. He hadn't wanted to make an issue of talking to her in front of Kinera Kran. And his conversation with the older woman had given him information about her husband – not least that he had definitely been in the village last night as well as the night the car went in the river.

As soon as they were far enough away not to be heard by Kinera, Campbell asked, 'What does she mean calling her ex-husband a murderer?'

'I think she must mean her son, Inspector,' said Bonita. The fringed scarf tied around her waist touched his arm. 'The child died when he was two. I don't know how, but she blames Kenneth. She's been very upset by the death in the river. She only told me about her son yesterday. I have always forgiven her for drinking. Now I understand it.'

'Do you think the boy's death was his fault?'

'How should I know, Inspector?'

He looked at her steadily until she said,

'OK, I do know him. Kenneth was with me the night Graham Pleasance was killed, Inspector. That is what you want to know, isn't it? I know it is a wicked thing. I was in bed with him at the time the car went in the river. I heard Kinera shout out and I went to her studio. Kenneth left then. Inspector, having an affair with her divorced husband was so exciting. He is a little naughty, you know? And the – how do you say – the deception has thrilled me. He has been in the house and she has never known.'

She bent down and picked two ripe wrinkled strawberries, 'These are sweet, more so than the perfect forms,' she said offering Campbell one and eating the other.

As he bit into it he saw Bonita smile. 'I go back now,' she said.

The large figure of Janet Sparrow on her bicycle riding up to the field caught his interest and he was relieved to turn away from Bonita Arlotte.

There he was. Janet had been hoping to run into him while on her various afternoon errands about the village. This afternoon she'd been asked to order some extra strawberries for the village post office. She'd caught Campbell up at Drain Farm early this morning on her post round. He hadn't seemed to listen to her when she'd tried to explain about her cousin, but she thought it was worth another try.

He wasn't how you'd expect a policeman to be. He looked like an over-sized squirrel, the way he seemed to hunch himself over his thoughts. And there was something about the way he looked. He was a man who could understand sadness, she was sure. It was the way he gazed out of those nut-coloured eyes into your soul.

"That Arlotte girl swings her hips like a whore," she thought as she saw the girl prance back to her seat next to Kinera Kran. "I'd love to know what that Kran woman's up to with all her letters," she added as she covered the remaining distance between the farmhouse and the strawberry field.

Placing her bicycle across Campbell's path she blurted out, 'I must speak to you about my aunt.'

While she took a breath she heard Campbell say, 'Ah, good afternoon, Miss Sparrow.'

'Well, she's not really my aunt. She's my cousin really, but because she's so much older I call her "Auntie",' she explained in a rush. Then she had to pause to allow a jet to pass over. 'My grandfather and her father were brothers. Auntie Maggie was under age, so my grandfather had to give his permission for her to marry Jon Norrice. I wasn't born, of course, but you learn these things, don't you? She's had a funny life. Her father was killed when the river burst its banks sixty odd years ago. There was a rumour that she and Norrice had a baby, and that it died.'

'What happened to Jon Norrice?' asked Campbell. He was frowning and seemed to be listening intently.

'He disappeared, so they say,' said Janet.

'What did this man, Jon Norrice, look like?'

'Of course I never saw him. I did see a wedding picture of them on Auntie Maggie's dressing table when I was a girl. He was blond and square faced, handsome – like one of them pictures of Greek Gods.'

'Now, Miss Sparrow, what has this to do with my present investigations?'

'That's why she won't speak to anyone, Inspector. She saw something that night with her cats. She's in danger. I know she is. Please come and talk to her. I'm sure you could get her to talk to you.'

Janet watched Campbell sucking strawberry juice off his index finger until he said, 'We tried to talk to her earlier without success. But I'll certainly come and see her with you. Though I must have a word with my sergeant first.'

She waited for Campbell while he spoke with the young fair policeman and the bearded one with the clipboard. The fair one seemed to be doing a lot of talking until another police car came up and parked behind the one already there. A woman got out. She was dressed in a short sleeved jacket and pleated skirt and her blond hair was neatly folded on the back of her head. She approached the group of policemen.

The smart woman spoke to the men for a few minutes. Then they all got into the cars. DI Campbell got into the passenger seat of the car the woman had arrived in while she took the driver's seat. The bearded man got in behind them. And the tall fair haired policeman went on his own to the car Janet had seen parked next to the weighing shed when she'd pedalled up to the Inspector. Before leaving, the blond one pulled a parcel of papers out of his car and passed them through DI Campbell's window.

The wheels churned the gravel. The policemen were gone. Janet sighed and went across to the farmer to order strawberries for the post office.

Campbell wondered what he was doing listening to Janet Sparrow's gossip, and yet he felt that what Maggie Norrice could tell him was important. But before he went to see the old girl he would just have to check what Parnold had found out from the farmer.

'He was told the soil sample was routine,' said Parnold when he reached him. 'He didn't know whether the samples had been sent in. The whole business had worried him though, because he did know part of the farm had been a munitions dump during the war. He doesn't look the murdering sort, Sir.'

Campbell looked at the pink face and the gut hanging over the belted trousers. The farmer was wearing his harvest smile, which embraced all before him. He certainly didn't look like a murderer today.

His thoughts were interrupted by WDC Jenner saying that she'd been trying to find them.

'We've been talking to Mr Sturning at the pub,' she said. 'On the night of the murder Bonita Arlotte was in there with a tall blond man who looked like someone called Eira Dublin. There was also a Chinese girl. She was with a very tall lanky girl.'

'Was there no Graham Pleasance?' asked Campbell.

'No,' said Jenner.

In his mind he ticked off the people she described. The man who looked like Dublin was Kenneth Kran. The Chinese girl was Sheena Kiljames. And the tall lanky girl, could that be Christine Pleasance? But there must be hundreds of lanky girls about. But if it was her, she had known Sheena, when she'd said she didn't.

'I think we'd better go and see Christine Pleasance,' he said. He was about to say something else when he was distracted by Alec Gowan fidgeting. He was almost hopping from one leg to the other.

'Do you want the toilet?' asked Parnold.

'Are you going to arrest someone?' asked Gowan.

'Have you got a box on the form for it?' asked Campbell.

'As a matter of fact, I have,' replied Gowan.

Campbell turned from the man and, while he rubbed strawberry juice off his thumb, he said, 'Parnold, I want to know as much as possible about Kenneth Kran and Eira Dublin. And I want a watch set up on Kenneth Kran's lorries.'

Parnold's face looked as if it had turned into rubber. Campbell shrugged his shoulders, OK so it was a lot of work. 'Give me the rest of Graham Pleasance's papers. I'll finish looking through them,' he said.

Campbell tapped Jenner's arm. They'd got as far as the Wet Goose. 'Turn back to the farm,' he said. Jenner frowned at him. He didn't want to explain, but to get her to cooperate and not just obey her senior officer he would have to tell her something. 'Maggie Norrice was a witness to the incident on the bridge. Christine Pleasance and her possible untruths will have to wait.' That sounded reasonable, but he knew that it was partly the challenge of talking to someone who'd not spoken to another human being for so many years.

There was a shuffle of papers behind him. He would have to think of a way of getting rid of Alec Gowan and his blasted clipboard.

Chapter 11

Maggie Norrice leant against the inside of the front door holding the key in her hands. She prayed Janet would go away. The pestering girl had been shouting through the window and now she was just inches away from her on the other side of the door. Maggie's body was wracked with sobbing and weak from wakefulness. All those memories she'd thought were lost had found her, and destroyed her.

At least now she could hate Jon Norrice for what he'd done to her. But that seemed such a small crime against her own wickedness. The guilt tapped inside her head like Janet tapping on the door. Then she said, 'Janet, I've murdered someone.' Her heart shook inside her chest. 'And now I'm going to die for it.' She shut her mouth tight. She'd said too much and it couldn't be unsaid.

'Auntie, you saw someone killed. That's all. You saw the car go off the bridge the other night. There's nothing to be frightened of if you tell the police what you saw. They can catch the man and you'll be safe.'

'Can policemen catch ghosts?'

'Auntie,' came the pleading voice.

'I got to tell the police about another murder.' Then she whispered, 'The one I committed.' And she said to herself, 'Only when I've done that can my father rest in peace.'

'Open the door, Aunt.'

She did as she was told. But Janet was not on her own. There was a Scotsman calling himself DI Campbell and a blond woman that she could see. DI Campbell made wheedling noises about the weather, the river and the wild flowers as he came in and headed towards a seat. He said he'd met Janet at the fruit farm. This thin bowed branch of a man was followed in by the blond woman. She was in her late twenties or early thirties and introduced herself as WDC Jenner. Maggie noticed her laced shoes pick their way through to stand by the Inspector. Then Janet tried to come in.

'I don't want you here,' she said more sharply than she meant to. Then she saw a bearded man behind her cousin. 'What do you want?' she asked.

'Look after Janet for me, Alec,' said the Inspector from beside her. He had arrived there without her noticing him. The man called Alec frowned for a moment, then waved his clipboard. Inspector Campbell closed the door.

Maggie felt calm. 'I didn't want Janet to hear the things I have to say.' But talking felt strange. The words were stiff and not like thoughts, somehow they didn't come out how she wanted them to. They sounded angry instead of confidant.

'I had a son, Inspector,' she said, seating herself on the shabby chair next to the range. 'He died.' She straightened her back and kept her eyes focused on the far corner of the hearth. 'He was asleep in the garden. I'd put the pram in the shade. My husband, Jon, found him, Inspector, while I was hanging washing.'

'Tell me about it, Mrs Norrice,' said DI Campbell.

'That's it. I killed him.' Maggie fiddled with a buttonhole in her cardigan.

'Jon Norrice?'

'My son.'

'I've learnt something of you, Mrs Norrice,' said DI Campbell. 'I know your mother was hit by an aeroplane crashing in a local field during the war and that your father was drowned during floods some years later. You married a man working in a gang on the banks to try and prevent those same floods.'

Maggie pretended to count the cat hairs on her trousers. How could he know so much about her already?

'I've looked into the history of the fens, and the floods. Did you know there were prisoners of war in the gangs working on the riverbanks?'

Maggie stopped and looked at him and nodded. 'The war was over. They were waiting to go home,' she said. She stared into his nut-brown eyes. They were steady and searching. She looked away quickly.

'Did he want to stay? Is that why you married him?'

'I just married him. That was all.' But it explained his dislike of her and yet his determination to marry her. She hadn't even thought about it until now. She'd just assumed all men were as hateful as her father. 'He wouldn't let me see anyone,' she said. 'I had the baby on my own.' She rubbed her nose on her sleeve and the inspector passed her a handkerchief.

'He told me I'd killed my father,' she continued. 'I couldn't swim. You see? I wanted to help him but he pulled me away and...' she couldn't say the words. For more than sixty years she'd thought what had happened had been her fault. She'd heard the word on television that described what happened. It was an alien word to her. It was a word she could not think let alone speak.

The Jenner woman was clucking and patting her shoulder. It ought to annoy her but she found it strangely soothing.

'I can't stop crying – not since the memory came back of what happened to my son.'

'Start with what you saw on the bridge,' said DI Campbell, 'the other night when the car crashed into the river.'

'I saw a man on the bridge.' Maggie wiped her eyes. 'I thought it was my husband, or his ghost. It looked so much like him, but he would be very old now. He was a good bit older than me. This man was younger than that: a man in his late middle-age. It wasn't till I saw him again last night outside Kinera Kran's house that I realised my son would be that sort of age, if he'd lived. I thought my father had sent my son's ghost to haunt me.' She glanced up at Jenner. The policewoman was writing furiously into her notebook. Such notions sounded silly looking at the woman's sensible face and soft but no nonsense suit.

'Did you ever see your son's body, Mrs Norrice?' asked DI Campbell.

Maggie shut her eyes and saw herself being pushed by Jon Norrice towards the pumping drain. 'You've killed our son,' he said over and over again. She was shouting, 'No,' and scrambling to her feet, trying to get to the pram. But he kept knocking her down. The bank of the drain dropped her finally at the edge of the water. She could hear the pumps and see the heat haze coming out of the chimney above her as she fought his hands about her throat. While thrashing her limbs she lost the air in her lungs and her mind swallowed the memory of her son. Somehow she'd spluttered her way out and clung to the bank for hours. She couldn't even remember getting rid of the pram or the baby's clothes. Had she spoken what she'd seen in her head? She wasn't sure; so she wiped her sweated hands on her trousers.

'No,' she said in answer to the inspector's question. 'He attacked me. I suppose he took Matthew's body with him. I couldn't even remember having a baby until last night. And Jon never came back.'

'Mrs Norrice, do you think your son could still be alive?'

'How?'

'Supposing Jon Norrice only told you the baby was dead and attacked you, not because of anything you'd done, but to get you out of the way while he took the baby?'

'Why?'

'He'd got what he wanted. He could now stay in England, so he moved out. But he wanted his child, so he took him. Can I see a picture of your husband, Mrs Norrice?'

Maggie couldn't quite believe that the man she'd given her life to, wretched though it was, could just leave her and take her child. Why? She pulled her felted picture from her pocket and gave it to him. She thought she saw the inspector's face change in recognition.

'The man on the bridge, the man last night, was it my son?'

'Most unlikely, Mrs Norrice,' said Campbell. 'You haven't committed a crime. You have witnessed one. It has disturbed and frightened you. The man on the bridge just looks a bit like your husband as you remember him.'

Maggie glanced around the room. The shaft of light from the window caught the dust layer over the chairs.

'Perhaps Janet will stop with you?' suggested Jenner.

Maggie nodded. In a matter of minutes this strange Scotsman had challenged her ghosts and sent them away. And now he stood by the door rocking backwards onto his heels and forwards onto the balls of his feet.

WDC Jenner stretched her shoulders in the sunshine as they walked back to the car with Alec Gowan three paces behind them. Campbell needed sorting out, she decided. OK so he'd found out what the man on the bridge looked like. He'd shown her the picture. He was blond, broad faced. But the old woman's eyesight must be dickey. She kept squinting at everything. She could have seen anybody up there in the dark that night. And last night, who the heck had she seen last night next to Kinera Kran's house?

'You don't know her son's alive, Sir,' she said. 'And you guessed that stuff about her husband. Her baby could have been dead. And that person she saw last night and on the bridge could easily have been anybody. It could even have been a strongly built female. You can't trust the old girl's eyesight. Did you see her squint? I bet she's never been for an eye test.'

'It was dark in there except for the shaft of light from the window. She'd been crying.' Campbell glanced behind at Alec Gowan who said, 'You must forget I'm here.'

'But you're right,' said Campbell. 'We really must go and see Christine Pleasance and find out if what she has been telling us is all a fairy tale. And afterwards you can chase up the history of Jon Norrice.'

Chapter 12

Campbell looked out from the hide across the blue field to the emerald pasture beyond. He watched police frogmen searching the water and the body of Sheena Kiljames being taken away. Mr Lyle, the warden of the nature reserve, stood next to him. He offered Campbell his binoculars. The Inspector refused; he'd already been too close.

He hadn't wanted to find Sheena Kiljames like this. Her long black hair and creamy skin was already riddled with insects looking for an easy meal. A rat had gnawed at her foot.

'She wasn't found until this morning when the week-end volunteers went down on the wetlands to finish clearing the area she'd been working on during the week,' Mr Lyle explained.

Campbell felt the man's bulk fill the hide and wondered how such a man could cope with being huddled up in such a place for hours on end. 'Did no one see the television or the radio or papers? There was an appeal out for her whereabouts.'

'I certainly didn't,' said Lyle. 'Such rubbish in the media nowadays. Normally all I want to see and listen to is right here. But I've been away this week.' He looked down.

Alec Gowan was standing by the door. Campbell had tried to keep him out using the lack of space as an excuse, but he'd claimed to be small and jammed himself in such a way no one could get in or out without him saying, 'Just ignore me.'

Yesterday's trip to see Christine Pleasance had been a waste of time as she'd been out. They'd been on their way to see her this morning when the report of Sheena's body had come over the radio and the trip had been delayed again. Alec Gowan had dropped his papers over the back seat, and the draft coming through the open window had blown them about. Then he'd complained bitterly that he wasn't a policeman and he shouldn't be given jobs to do. Campbell hadn't liked to tell him that he'd asked him to look after Janet Sparrow to get rid of him.

When Parnold came in, he hissed at Gowan, 'You're in my way.'

'Aye, so I understand,' said Campbell to Lyle, at last replying to his statement about the events of this morning. The ladies over in the gift shop and tea room had already told him that Sheena must have been on her own over there because no one else had been around. She had popped her head round the door first thing that day, but they hadn't seen her since, which didn't surprise them, really, with her being so quiet. The access to the bird-watching area was some distance from the shop, which he soon found out for himself.

He knew routine questions would give routine answers – useful and limited – but he wanted the sort of questions, which would produce revealing answers. And these sorts of questions would not come with Gowan scrunched up by the door.

Parnold interrupted his thoughts by calling Campbell out of the room.

'Sir, Christine Pleasance is here,' said Parnold. 'She heard on the TV about the body being found. She wants to know who it is. Shall I send her home?'

'No, Parnold keep her here. I'll talk to her later, but I want to speak to the forensic people first.'

Campbell returned to the slatted wooden building and asked Lyle, 'I hope you don't mind if we borrow your office briefly?'

'Of course, help yourself,' replied Lyle.

Campbell slipped out with Lyle, leaving Gowan in the hide. Campbell thanked Lyle as they stood on the wooden landing outside the hide and he watched while the warden was escorted away from the crime scene by a uniformed policeman.

The steps at the back led out onto a grassy track screened from the reserve by dense willow hedging. This was the way the murderer would have come, thought Campbell. But then there was only one access across to the wetlands, and this was it.

Remembering the bruises he'd seen earlier around Sheena's neck made him think of Maggie Norrice and her fight with her husband. She'd spoken as if in a dream when she'd told him about her baby. Could there possibly be a stronger link between this old woman's lost son and these murders than a slight similarity in features between the possible murderer and her husband? No, surely not.

'These women at the café,' said Parnold, 'reckoned the warden's been down in London all week at some conference or other. They didn't see anyone come or go. It's the quiet season here. People mostly come to see the birds that winter here.'

'Aye, so I understand,' said Campbell. Mary Brown's bulk covered by her white overalls had caught his attention. Her warm features were grinning while the sound of her talking to one of her charges came across to him like the purr of an oversized cat.

'Found out who's done it, then?' he asked her as her colleague slid back through the gap in the willow hedge.

'That joke is wearing thin, Campbell,' said Mary Brown.

'Is there any physical evidence to link this murder with Graham Pleasance's death?'

'Not yet.' Her voice told him he was a silly boy. And she turned back to the van. 'We will have to check for fibres.'

'Have you found anything?'

'Yes,' she sounded slightly irritated. 'She seems to have cut her own boot with the sickle. She put up a fight.'

Campbell noted the pride in her voice for this once beautiful girl. 'Anything else?' he asked quietly.

'There's a house type key,' she asked not bothering to turn around. 'You can have it as soon as we've finished with it.'

Campbell nodded at Christine Pleasance to sit down opposite him in the sanctuary warden's office. 'Hot enough for you?' he asked conversationally.

'Who is it – the body? I heard it on the news.' Her height folded easily onto a chair while she placed her leather handbag awkwardly on her knee.

He saw Parnold twitch and Gowan fumble with his pen. The room had thin walls; he would check his voice.

'Why?' he asked. She gave no reply so even more quietly he added, 'Where were you the night your father was killed?'

'I've already told you. I was at home in Cambridge,' she replied softly.

Parnold was clicking his thumbnail against a filing cabinet. Campbell gave him a "Shut up" look and said to Christine, 'I don't think you were.'

'Why?' There was a guarded check in her voice.

'Come, Miss Pleasance, surely you realised such an incident would not go unnoticed in a small pub like the Wet Goose at Sparrow Bank. You would have been better off meeting Sheena Kiljames in one of the towns unless you had a reason to be at Sparrow Bank the night your father died.'

Christine Pleasance looked at Campbell. He stared back, penetrating. She lowered her eyes. 'I went to tell her to stay away from my father. It would kill my mother if she knew about them. The longer their relationship carried on the more likely she was to find out. I had to stop that.'

'Even by killing your father?' asked Parnold.

'Miss Pleasance,' said Campbell catching her attention as she floundered from Parnold's question, 'Tell me what happened.'

'I told her to stay away but she lied through her pearly teeth.' Christine's voice died. When she spoke again it was a little louder than before. 'She said nothing was going on between them. I didn't believe her. I got angry and then said that she already had a lover and it wasn't my father.'

'Did she tell you who it was?' asked Campbell.

Christine shook her head. 'I suppose you won't tell me who the body is you've found.'

'Campbell said nothing for a moment then he said, 'Please answer Sergeant Parnold's question: did you kill your father?'

'No, I couldn't do that. How could I take him from my mother? She loves him. I could never have caused the pain she's in now.' Her voice was stronger but still not loud.

'Could it be better than the pain of betrayal?' Campbell's Edinburgh accent made the words clear despite their quietness.

'No, Inspector, I'm not that stupid.' Christine looked from Campbell to Parnold and back again. 'It's her, isn't it? And you think I killed my father and then Sheena in a fit of jealousy?'

'It is a possibility, Miss Pleasance,' said Campbell. He jiggled the adjustment levers on his seat. He was getting pins and needles in his right foot. 'You didn't tell us, Miss Pleasance, that your father was involved in examining and testing contaminated lands. You might know we would find out such a thing quite quickly.'

'He never told me,' said Christine.

'Indeed, Miss Pleasance? Earlier you told us that your father told you all about his work, so why should he leave out such an important area?' Campbell leaned forward. 'And it was in this area that Sheena Kiljames was working with him. Why if you had nothing to hide did you not tell us these things?'

'Because you would have asked Mother about it,' Christine conceded with a drop of her head. 'Then she would have known. And he's dead. Don't you understand, she's already lost him? Please don't destroy her memories.'

'But you did mention that Sheena Kiljames said she had another lover, Miss Pleasance.' Campbell kept his body still and his voice level.

'So what? That mightn't have stopped her. It doesn't some people. And I know my father never told Mother about Sheena Kiljames. What does that tell you?' Christine's whole body twisted as she spoke. Each word was wrestled with and came out choked.

'We called on you yesterday, but you were out. Could you tell me where you were?' asked Campbell.

'Out getting groceries. Why?' This time the question was edged with anger.

'Would you be pleased if I told you Sheena Kiljames was dead?'

'She deserves it if anybody does but it's pointless now. My father's already dead. If he was still alive then it would be worthwhile. It is her, isn't it?'

'Yes,' said Campbell. He watched her face work. Her temper was cut back by this. Was it confusion or guilt?

She fiddled with the strap on her bag. When she looked up he could see her confidence had returned. She asked, 'Don't you see who's behind all this? It's got to be Sheena's other lover. Find out who he is. He must have seen what I saw and become jealous and murdered them both.' Christine grasped Campbell's arms and shook them. He was surprised at her strength. 'You must,' she insisted.

Clearing his throat Campbell said, 'Miss Pleasance, you seem a little overly involved with your parents for a young woman of your age. Do you have a boyfriend?'

'I don't have to answer that.' This time her reply was shouted at them and she rose so quickly from her seat that she knocked it over. Campbell saw the woman in the shop outside the office look up from her stock-taking as Christine pushed her way out of the office past Parnold and Gowan.

As the shop door swung shut Campbell heard Parnold say to Gowan that she was probably a 'dyke'. So he felt obliged to say, 'Do you say that because you don't fancy her, or because she doesn't fancy you? And I'm not sure her sexuality has a bearing on this case, are you?' But it wasn't really a question.

Parnold replied, 'Sir,' and Campbell was pleased to exercise his stiff leg as far as the car.

The tiny terraced house in Ouse Crossing opened up its contents to the police with the key that had been found on Sheena Kiljames. Campbell had noted that nothing at the tent site or on her related to any person but herself. They'd been able to contact her next of kin through her work but this search was focussed on Sheena's supposed lovers.

Campbell was relieved to be rid of Alec Gowan for the afternoon. He'd complained that he thought he was getting a migraine, apologised and gone home. But Campbell didn't like looking through other people's private things. Each china dog or silvered frame with a picture of a bird seemed to contain Sheena's presence. He stood in the middle of the room while the team searched. He recognised one of them.

'Garden?' he asked a WPC with frizzy brown hair poking out of her uniform hat. He regretted giving Parnold and Jenner other jobs to do. But he had committed himself, and so them, to finding out the backgrounds of Kenneth Kran the refuse contractor, Eira Dublin with his food factory and even Jon Norrice – the cat lady's long lost husband. How strange these men should look so alike and all turn up in a tiny village like Sparrow Bank. He wanted to know about them – even Kenneth Kran with his alibi of Bonita Arlotte on the night of Graham Pleasance's murder. He was sure his activities were, at best, irregular.

'Sir,' said Garden.

'What do you think?' he asked.

'There's nothing, Sir. It's strange. If she had a man there would be something. Not necessarily a letter, but he might leave an item of clothing or she might have a momento. She doesn't even have any jewellery.' WPC Garden turned back to her work and Campbell stepped out onto the front step wondering if Graham Pleasance and Sheena Kiljames had really been lovers. Were they looking for something of his or something that belonged to another man? He waggled his head to stretch his neck.

The neighbour he'd met the other morning getting the milk in stuck her head over the fence. There was no grief in her face though Sheena's demise had been given out on the lunch time news now that her family in

Ireland had been informed.

'Didn't see much of her really,' she offered. 'Always out. But then young girls always are these days.' Her tight grey curls had a blue tinge to them he hadn't noticed the first time he'd seen her.

'Boyfriends?' he asked conversationally.

The woman's face brightened with the thought of gossip and then darkened again in disappointment. 'No. Not one. She came here just to sleep and then not every night.'

'Is that right?' asked Campbell.

She brightened again. 'I can hear every sound in that house. When the front door opens or closes you can hear it in my living room.' The neighbour strained to see inside Sheena's house. 'You lot won't be long, I hope, I take a nap every afternoon.'

'We're nearly finished, madam. I've just got to go and check on something. Goodbye.' With this he went back inside to ask Garden if any keys had been found. She said they had and they were on the table with some photographs she thought she might look at.

The photographs were family snaps: an Irish father with an oriental wife standing with their son and daughter in front of the Kiljames pharmacy; a little Sheena on a dun coloured pony; Sheena's brother on a bicycle. The keys were on two rings. On one was a bird, on the other a fish. Campbell found the bird keys fitted the house doors but he could find no match for the fish keys.

'Is this really necessary on a Saturday evening, Inspector,' complained the squat laboratory manager. Campbell had not only checked the fish keys against the laboratory keys but he was checking each key in every lock.

'Aye,' he said, 'It is.' He was tired himself now and his voice only just gave the illusion of police efficiency. He raised his eyebrows to keep his eyes open a little wider. His breathing was quiet like someone already in a deep sleep. The keys wouldn't fit. That made it unlikely she was coming back here for any reason – doctoring results or making checks of her own. Nor was she using it as a rendezvous with a lover.

The evening sunlight dazzled through the slatted blinds and glinted on the glass of the fume cupboard. Campbell blinked. It was time to stop. His investigations were getting him nowhere. And he knew who to blame for that: the tick box man.

Chapter 13

Kinera Kran chucked the ball of paper towards the bin. She never wrote letters in her studio. She pushed away her laptop. This was a sanctuary of paint and canvas. But her house seemed no longer to be her own with Bonita Arlotte always rushing to help. Two-faced bitch. Didn't she know her little game was as obvious as her hips?

'Kenneth uses her like he used me,' she told her painting of the river. In it the water was frozen. She'd never really seen it like this, but for her this was the truth. She'd had enough of her Spanish companion and she was going to make her leave.

'Bon,' Kinera shouted at the door.

'Coming,' came the lingering reply. The girl came in. The movement of her body seemed to fill the room.

Kinera took a long paintbrush from a pot and snapped it in two and said, 'Sit.' She placed her on a stool and surrounded her with a drape. She stood back and looked.

'Are you going to paint me?' asked Bonita.

'I don't paint portraits. People are only part of a greater landscape,' she replied.

'Why then?' asked Bonita.

'I want to take a look at the whore bitch who likes to play games. And what games did he want to play?'

'It wasn't like that.'

Kinera could see Bonita was lying so she asked, 'What was it like, Bon, dear?'

'OK, so you know about Kenneth and me. It didn't mean anything.' Bonita pouted. 'I always knew he was yours.'

'I don't own him. We are divorced. You told me that yourself not so long ago. Why should I worry about whom you screw?' Kinera picked up a hooked craft knife and started slashing the ends of the fabric wrapped around her beautiful, deceitful Bon. 'But why did you do it in my house?'

'You're drunk,' said Bonita defensively.

Kinera saw Bon's espadrilled feet shrink back from her blade but she felt her hot dark eyes glare at her. She was angry and a little frightened; good. 'Your lack of English has gagged you. Is that all you can say?' Kinera watched her hand off the drape and kick it away before making for the door.

'You are crazy.' Bonita gestured at her head.

But Kinera could see Bon was unsettled by her challenge. 'You always know men are cheating when they mention rules,' said Kinera. She waited for Bon to stop and grip the door surround to control herself. 'Kenneth likes his rules. I saw him with some other woman the night the car went in the river. I don't know what you told the police but I can bet anything from the way they were behaving he wasn't with you that night.'

'He was with me. We made love until the car went in the river in my bed, in your house.'

'Women have to create, men have to play.' Kinera smiled to herself, as the studio door slammed shut behind Bonita. Back, fingering her writing paper she said, 'And I've written his other woman a letter.'

Campbell savoured for a moment the disorder of his cottage kitchen. There were nearly every cup and saucer he'd ever seen in his home stuck together on the draining board. Pots and pans were leaning against each other on the cooker. He breathed in. The smell of a tea long eaten coated his nose and tongue. Something exotic.

He heard the sound of teenage laughter and a voice that always reached inside him. Its gentle firm tones were placing, checking pondering.

When he entered the living room his fourteen-year-old son, Edmund, and thirteen-year-old daughter, Victoria, were dancing to vibrant music. He wracked his brain for forgotten birthdays, and failed. There were two or three more – in his present state of exhaustion he couldn't decide exactly how many – teenagers thrust together on the settee. One of them was fiddling with a games machine which made noises that caught Campbell in the back of the neck.

He raised his arms slightly. He wanted to say that he couldn't think.

He felt like a toddler lost in a supermarket until his wife, Margaret, steered him upstairs to bed.

A bright round moon filled the quiet room with light when he awoke. He looked at his wife. How could two women with the same name be so different? He thought about the way she looked when she stitched a wall hanging, did her business accounts or got the children to tidy their rooms. And then there was the cat lady, thirty years older. She'd allowed herself to fall away from life, bullied by people who were already dead and gone.

His brain had switched itself on so he got out of bed and pulled on some old clothes. In the hallway he noted that the back bedroom door didn't quite hold in the smell of new paint. He decided to stopper up the gap under the door with newspaper when he'd finished.

The acrid fumes seemed to clear his head as he worked the roller across the wall, or, perhaps, it was just the effect of being out of Alec Gowan's efficiency shadow.

He had three possibilities for the man on the bridge: Eira Dublin, Kenneth Kran and Christine Pleasance. They all had the opportunity: Eira was babysitting his sleeping children not far from Sparrow Bank; Kenneth had been seen in the Wet Goose with Bonita Arlotte; and Christine Pleasance had been there with Sheena Kiljames.

And Sheena: her time of death had been difficult to define. The pathologist said he would be able to get it down to the day when he'd done some more tests but it would be nearly impossible at present to give a time. Campbell remembered feeling rather clever and looking for her watch. He'd hoped it had become waterlogged and stopped. In fact it was waterproof and was still counting days, hours, minutes and seconds. And it would be nearly impossible for Eira, Kenneth or Christine to have an alibi for a whole day.

He was sure the same person had murdered both Sheena and Graham. The connection between their jobs was obvious. If only Mary Brown could confirm the link between their deaths with some sort of evidence.

Now motives. Christine Pleasance certainly had one even if she cares to deny it. She was obviously jealous of Sheena and her father. But if she was the murderer wasn't it unnecessary for her to come and ask who the body was? Why ask anyway? To make herself look innocent?

Kenneth Kran was involved with all the things Graham and Sheena were employed to prevent or control. But he had an alibi for the time of the bridge accident.

Eira Dublin didn't seem to have a motive. There was some vague link with Kinera Kran who'd sent letters of complaint about his products, and that was all.

There was some point he was missing. But when he thought really hard all he could see was Alec Gowan ticking boxes.

'What's up?' asked Margaret opening the door a fraction.

'Thinking.'

'About what?'

'Efficiency.'

She laughed at him.

'Och, it's this consultant. He's driving me crazy. I just can't think straight when he's around.'

'You wimp.'

'I beg your pardon?'

'You heard.'

'Aye.'

'Wash that paint off you and come back to bed.' She smiled.

He did as he was told.

Later his nightmare returned: he was under water looking up and, somehow, he could still breathe.

Maggie Norrice took off her cardigan. The daytime heat had taken until night to penetrate the grimy curtains and the heavy doors. Even the quarry-tiled floor seemed less cold.

She dragged the table the short distance to the side of the room near the scullery, climbed up and looked at the hook in the ceiling. She pulled on it.

Her father's ghost had disappeared. And the ghost of her son hadn't been a ghost at all according to that Scottish Inspector. After speaking to him she'd realised the figure on the bridge the night the car'd gone into the river was a man. And the spirit that touched her last night next to Kinera Kran's house was human. The tension created by her belief in these ghosts had kept her going defiantly – and now they were gone.

Janet had been almost more difficult to get rid of. She'd told her to go home, she was all right and she needed to be on her own to think it through. Her cousin had only left when she'd allowed her to take some dirty linen away with her to wash.

Even in confessing to the police, she'd been wrong. Her father's ghost had goaded her into believing that was what she should do. He'd tricked her and made her do what he wanted. He'd always managed to do that, except when Jon Norrice had taken her over, for almost a year.

She'd only loved Jon Norrice because that was all she'd had to love, and she'd hated him in the same pulse. It hadn't all been his fault. She'd trapped him. No, she corrected herself, he was evil. He had used her body because it was there. But hadn't she asked for it to be used – used, not... She still couldn't even think the word.

Now her father's ghost was gone. And she didn't have to stay alive to spite him.

What had she done, speaking to people? She'd given her son to the police. She would never have told the police if she hadn't thought the sightings to be unreal because she thought she'd killed her baby son. If only she'd realised he was alive.

There was some rope in the shed. As she opened the door and flashed her light round one of her cats came and rubbed itself around her legs. She went in, leaving the cat outside. Janet would look after them. She rubbed her nose and was suddenly aware of tears storming down her face. She made them stop.

Shaking the rope free from its coil disturbed dust and an owl, which flew through a gap in the roof. Maggie barely flinched. She had no reason to be scared any more.

Back in the house she pondered sometime over the knot. She couldn't make a noose and wondered if a slipknot would be effective. It might take longer to die, she decided. That wasn't a problem.

Letting the loop hang down she wrapped the rope around the hook and then secured it to one of the stairs. She leaned back on her heals and congratulated herself on her handiwork.

Having pushed the table back to its original position she replaced it with a chair. Maggie decided against a note. She'd been long enough without explaining herself to start now. She tightened the rope about her neck and kicked the chair away. She felt her body fall and tried not to breathe. Death had seemed so inviting. Yet, when she tried to think of the river and the hours of pleasure it had given her – with its slow waters, swans and changing colours – in preparation for death, life did not seem so bad. And it was so difficult to die. Her body craved for air until she gasped. The rope notched tighter. It hurt. She could feel all the insides of her neck being crushed together. This was no more than she deserved, she told herself. But how much longer would it take?

The rope, above her, creaked. There was a splitting, tearing sound, and she was falling.

The quarry tiles were hard and her neck bruised. She loosened the knot. With death now further from her, she cried, miserable at her failure, and swore at the rope for being rotten and breaking when it had nearly done its job. Then she started to laugh at how funny she must look.

'You almost got me, you old sod,' she said to her father wherever he might be. 'Your ghost may've gone, but you're still trying to get me. I know it. I was saved. And I've had a good look at death now. And, though I'll take it when it comes, I in't going to look for it.' Her broad accented voice still sounded strangled to her. She laughed. She couldn't remember the last time she'd laughed so much. It was all the laughter she hadn't had put together. She dried the tears of mirth from her eyes with the sleeve of her cardigan and checked her bruises. She was still rubbing herself when Janet came in.

'What have you been doing, Auntie?' she asked.

Maggie felt her check for broken bones and saw the poor woman's face haggard with worry for her. 'I'm all right,' she told her cousin. 'The rope was rotten.'

'Why are you doing this?' asked Janet.

'I saw my son.'

'You should be pleased, not hanging yourself.'

'I told the police he was on the bridge the night the car went in the river.'

'You kept me outside when you spoke to them.'

'I know,' said Maggie regretting her lack of trust towards Janet – and yes she was over forty, not an eleven-year-old child. And she'd looked after her all these years. 'The police said that I saw someone who looked like my husband, not my son, or his ghost. Then they said my son could still be alive.'

'We could find this son of yours,' said Janet. 'What does he look like?'

'He looks like the man on the bridge,' said Maggie. Was the girl deaf or what? Hadn't she just told her he looked like her husband? Perhaps she couldn't remember the wedding photograph she saw when she was eleven? 'Fair hair, strong build,' she added.

'I've just realised,' said Janet, her worried lines deepening. 'We can't go looking for him right now. We could run into the murderer by mistake. We will have to let the police find him first and then we can start looking for your son.'

Maggie felt her hand being patted. She winced. The shout of one of her cats at the door gave her an excuse to take her hand back.

'Let's walk along the riverbank, Aunt Maggie. It will clear your head.'

Maggie allowed herself to be walked and as she breathed in the cooler outside air she decided that as soon as Janet was out of the way doing her post round on Monday she would start looking for her son.

Chapter 14

Campbell would have preferred to do this job at home or in the car – anywhere but in the office where superiors could invade his thoughts, the telephone could not be ignored and the paperwork spilled out of the 'In' tray. He was often tempted to pick it all up and dump it in the grey metal bin by his desk.

While he stared at the remaining Graham Pleasance papers, Alec Gowan sat behind his left shoulder. He couldn't help thinking that this squat gnome-like stance was as intrusive as the red and green concrete man his children had bought him five years ago, which he'd tried to hide in the shrubbery. However, the efficiency expert's silence was incomplete, unlike a garden ornament. Only the church bells calling folk to Sunday worship masked briefly the sound of breathing.

'I shall be doing this all morning,' he told Gowan. 'You can tick all your reading boxes and leave.'

"My study can have positive outcomes,' Alec Gowan said defensively.

Campbell's reply to this was a distracted frown. He looked back own at his desk.

He wondered about Graham Pleasance and his papers. Could his lack of organisation be because he was always leaping from one job to the next without any thought to tidying loose ends? Or could he have been hiding something in this muddle? Campbell decided that Graham Pleasance was just untidy.

There was a knock and Jenner entered, a folder under her arm. Campbell heard the air puffed out from Gowan's nostrils in triumph. Obviously talking with another officer involved ticking a different box.

Beckoning her to a seat beside his desk he settled his papers to one side and brought in front of him a large pad of paper. 'What have you got for me?' he asked.

'Can I tell you about Jon Norrice, Sir?' she asked.

'Aye,' said Campbell.

'Your guess was probably right,' she said. Campbell noted her wry grin. 'There were prisoners of war working along the river bank at that time.'

He didn't give her the benefit of a comment.

'There was only one that went missing that night. His name was Johan Stangarde. He was never recaptured. He was German, but it seems he was a bit of a thief in the prison camp, stole from his own comrades. I've even got his mug shot.'

'Well done. According to our witness the man on the bridge looked like this man.' This picture was better than the felted fragment of wedding photo Maggie Norrice had given him. There was no doubt in Campbell's mind that these two images were of the same square jawed man. The man that looked so like Kenneth Kran and Eira Dublin.

Before Campbell had finished looking at the photo of Johan Stangarde, Alec Gowan grunted as the door opened again. There'd been no knock this time. Parnold came in. He too was holding a folder.

'More background information for me, I hope?' asked Campbell.

Parnold pulled up a chair and replied, 'Kran's a public school boy.' His words sounded stiffened to Campbell with his local accent squeezed out to the edges of the sentence. 'His parents lived abroad, embassy people – distinguished, well off but not overly rich. He went to Oxford to read law, but never finished the course. He went straight into the refuse business and has made money ever since. His parents retired to Yorkshire. I don't know why we need all this guff, Sir? He was having it away with the Spanish bit the night Graham ended up in the river.'

Jenner muttered, 'Spanish Bit,' with disgust directed at Parnold. Campbell ignored her, but noticed that Parnold wanted to respond.

His colt was no war-horse. He looked tired. Parnold had known Graham Pleasance as a colleague and he was the sort of person who would be loyal to an older officer – if he'd gained his respect.

'Was Kenneth Kran adopted?' asked Campbell.

'No. I've seen his birth records.' Parnold's accent lapsed into Norfolk, shortening "seen" and lengthening "birth".

Making a note that Kinera Kran was not Maggie Norrice's son, Campbell asked, 'Have we still got a watch on his lorries?'

'Yes, Sir. It's you and me tonight.'

'On a Sunday?' asked Alec Gowan.

'If they're up to anything they'll definitely be up to it on a Sunday,' said Jenner.

'And Eira Dublin?' asked Campbell. He said it firmly to shut Alec Gowan up as well as his own officers. The efficiency expert seemed unable to keep quiet but Campbell wanted to prevent a squabble about a side issue.

'I don't know anything about his early life in Ireland.' Parnold was using his newsreader's voice again. 'I've asked the police over there but it may take a while. He seems to me to be a Cambridge University man, who bought shares in an ailing company and pulled it around. He made his money quickly and has bought other food factories as they've come available.'

'Aye,' said Campbell to encourage his colleague. He wrote on his pad that Eira Dublin could be Maggie Norrice's son, and wondered if such a thing was in any way relevant to the investigation. He noticed Jenner staring at Gowan behind him.

'He's got a separate company which is a land holding business.' Parnold pointed out the name in the folder he placed on the desk. Campbell read the sergeant's neat round handwriting. 'People seem to think he wants to consolidate his business by manufacturing all his different food products on one site.'

'I've seen that company name before,' said Campbell flicking through some papers he'd just read. 'It owns land which is heavily contaminated with all sorts of stuff.'

'At our briefing yesterday evening you said there was no point in anyone killing Graham Pleasance and Sheena Kiljames to avoid land being listed as contaminated because there would always be someone else to do the job,' said Parnold.

'Aye,' said Campbell in a way that said he might or might not've been wrong.

'Unless a delay would be enough for a land deal to go ahead?' suggested Jenner.

'Possibly,' said Campbell. 'WDC Jenner, I need you to go through these Pleasance papers again. Try and make connections between all these sample results. The man was so disorganised. Why he didn't get himself a few files, I'll never know.'

'He was a good policeman,' said Parnold.

'Aye,' said Campbell, 'I expect he was.' He pushed back his seat and went over to the window scratching dry paint off the back of his hand. 'I've got stiff sitting here,' he grumbled.

He stood watching the churchgoers walking back to their cars across the market place. He watched a woman trying to get into a car. She'd tried every key until someone came up to her and pointed out a similar vehicle a few spaces up. She went to it and the key worked perfectly.

'I might've thought of this yesterday afternoon when I first saw that fish key,' he said, 'if I hadn't been thinking about efficiency.'

'I wasn't about yesterday afternoon,' complained Alec Gowan. 'I had a migraine.'

'And you are meant to be invisible now,' said Campbell pleasantly, 'but I still see you.'

'I welcome Alec's study. I'm sure it will be of great benefit.' And, she gathered up the papers Campbell pointed out to her on his desk.

Gowan sighed and ticked another box.

The fish dangled from its chain while Campbell turned the key in the door. It opened easily. The tiny front room gave the impression of being dark green with the wellingtons, fishing brollies and waxed coats stood and hung about the room.

He wished he hadn't let himself into the little cottage at the base of the bridge at Sparrow Bank when he saw Eira Dublin sitting in the middle of the room weeping silently. Campbell touched his shoulder and Dublin looked around. His eyes were creamy with tears.

'I met Sheena while I was fishing a few months back,' he said. 'She was bird watching. When she spoke I was lost. Hearing her voice was like being a child again. My wife wouldn't let me have any connection with home. Sheena was Ireland to me.' Bringing his hands away from his chest he revealed the crumpled green jumper he'd been clutching. It was identical design and colour to the one Dublin was wearing.

Campbell looked more closely at the room's contents. Here were the photographs of Sheena and Eira Dublin together, and alone. Here was where her lover's clothes were kept. A pair of earrings dangled over the side of a dish on the mantelpiece.

'Do you know who killed her?' asked Campbell.

'No. If I did I would be there now tearing him apart limb by limb.'

'That wouldn't be advisable,' said Campbell, but he got no reply. 'I have to ask you some questions, some of them difficult.' Eira Dublin nodded. Campbell remembered Parnold. He would have liked him in on this but he'd already sent him across to see the people at the pub so he would have Gowan out of his way.

'Did Sheena come here the night Graham Pleasance was killed?' he asked.

'I wouldn't know, Inspector. I wasn't here. I was at home looking after my children.'

'Has anything been changed since you were here last?'

'No, I don't think so…' Eira's voice faded.

'Were Sheena Kiljames and Graham Pleasance lovers?'

Dublin laughed through his tears. 'No, Inspector. She told me about the rumours. She thought them funny. She may've been Irish but you can see she is, was, oriental. Most people of the world touch each other when they talk. It is only the British who don't.'

'I understand that you have a piece of land that's contaminated?'

'That's correct,' said Dublin. At the mention of his business Campbell noticed that his eyes dried and he became more alert through his distress. 'Arsenic, cyanide and toluene among others,' he added. 'Toluene will penetrate water pipes.'

'You were hoping to use the site to manufacture all your products?'

'Yes.'

'And now you'll have to sell it?'

'Yes, or have it cleaned up.'

'That would be expensive?'

'It's a cost I could have done without, yes.'

'It would be easier to sell it and start again on a new site?'

'I would lose heavily on what I paid for it. As contaminated land it is worse than valueless.'

'To sell it as uncontaminated you would have to delay Graham and Sheena from releasing their test result.'

'I wouldn't do such a thing.'

'Did you kill Graham Pleasance and Sheena Kiljames?'

'No. Inspector.' Eira Dublin looked shocked.

Campbell congratulated himself. Parnold could not've chased him any better than that. But he did not show his triumph. 'No?' he asked.

'Think it through, Inspector. If I wanted to do that I only had to ask Sheena to change the figures. She didn't do it because I didn't ask her.'

'Perhaps Sheena refused to change the lab results?'

'Inspector!' It was denial. 'I was going to have the site cleaned. Kenneth Kran was giving me a quote. You can check it all out with my secretary. Now please leave me alone.'

He could see the man wished to return to his crying. Campbell looked at the fish key ring. He wanted to give it to the square shape huddled on the floor, but he couldn't yet. He'd get Jenner to check Dublin's files first.

'Did you know where Sheena was?' he asked.

Eira did not move but said; 'If I had I would have told you.'

'Did you know she was in Sparrow Bank on the evening Graham Pleasance died?'

Still hunched over, he shook his head in reply.

Campbell left and closed the door and took a deep breath. Even here next to the fen river where there should be freshness the air was thick with heat. Midges swarmed. A tingling sensation marked the places the sun's rays had reached skin through his factor twenty sun tan cream.

He hooked his way up to the top of the bank and looked down at the water, bent over with one hand balancing and grabbing at the turf. The stillness belied the life the River Sparrow'd taken earlier in the week. Campbell remembered his dream: looking up through the water, being alive, seeing the surface, knowing it to be out of reach. Was that how Graham Pleasance and Sheena Kiljames had felt? Why had the murderer chosen water as his weapon? Was it because of its convenience on the fens, or was there another reason for this crime? His mind couldn't shake off Maggie Norrice and her son.

Janet Sparrow's plump arm waved at him from the other side of the river so he waited for her. She disappeared behind the far bank and reappeared at the bridge, which she walked over pushing her bike. Her bulk and the machine moved steadily over the tarmac road towards him.

'Auntie Maggie tried to kill herself,' she said as soon as she joined him at the top of the bank having left her bike at the bottom.

Examining her, Campbell found her bright blue eyes honest and demanding.

'Is she all right?' he asked.

'Well enough,' said Janet Sparrow. 'She's just bruised. She wouldn't see a doctor anyhow. It was what you said about her son being alive and all. She thought she'd betrayed him to you.' Janet rubbed the back of her hand across her forehead. 'Now she wants to find him.'

'Tell her 'No' for now, Miss Sparrow. It is too dangerous with this murderer about. Tell her to wait. The man only looks somewhat like her ex-husband; that is all. There may be absolutely no connection with her son. When this is all over I'll come and see her.'

'I told her, but I can't be with her all the time. I'm sure something is going to happen to her, Inspector.'

'I'll come and see her as soon as I can, Miss Sparrow.' Campbell's mind was being distracted by screeching female voices. The sound was bouncing around the riverbanks. It came from somewhere behind him and the voices were familiar.

Janet Sparrow said, 'I in't getting drawn into that. Goodbye, Inspector,' and she returned to her bike.

Turning, Campbell saw two women fighting in front of Kinera's house. Blue-black hair swung in an arc above the olive body of Bonita Arlotte as she crashed into the much taller Christine Pleasance. Christine buckled under the force and Bonita made a clutch at her hair. In turn, Campbell saw, as he slid down the bank, Christine grab a handful of black hair. Bonita was yelling in Spanish, her head tilted back by the pull. Christine grunted with effort.

Before Janet Sparrow and her bike reached the far side of the bridge, the wood and metal structure resounded with the pounding feet of Parnold and Gowan running from the direction of the Wet Goose. They arrived at the same time as Campbell at Kinera's garden gate. Parnold pulled the two women apart. He held one on each side of him. Bonita spat at Christine and continued to rant in Spanish until Parnold told her to shut up. Christine's face was scratched and she held a lock of black hair like a trophy. Gowan looked relieved that he was not asked to help. He seemed to be ticking several boxes at once.

'Now then, ladies,' said Campbell using his sharpest Edinburgh accent to bring them to order. 'What's going on?'

'Nothing now,' said Christine.

'Bitch!' yelled Bonita.

'I haven't made up my mind yet whether I ought to charge you with disturbing this peaceful Sunday afternoon. So I want the truth out of you two. Perhaps Mrs Kran can help us?'

'She's out,' said Bonita straightening her clothes. 'Kinera didn't want him, not really, so I took him.'

'He didn't love you,' said Christine. 'I had a letter this morning. It said he was still involved with this whore. It's a lie.' She screamed the last sentence at Bonita and tried to pull away from Parnold.

'They were in the pub together the evening your father died,' said Campbell.

'Kenneth did that to cover,' said Christine. 'I met him later in the car park. Bonita left him by his car and went home by herself. Kenneth Kran was with me that night not her.'

'All night?'

'Yes.'

'Why did he say he was with Bonita?'

'We didn't want it getting back to my family that we were together. He knew she would be stupid enough to back him whatever he said.'

'He didn't need anyone else,' said Bonita. 'I was enough for him.' Her dark eyes narrowed. 'What would he want with a girl like you – so man like.'

The two women started to struggle away from Parnold's grasp so Campbell felt obliged to take Bonita off him, and he said, 'We'll arrest these two, take them to the station, charge them and let them cool down before putting them on police bail.'

'Please,' said Christine, 'My letter.' Parnold released one of her hands so she could pass the open anonymous type written note to Campbell.

'Kinera sent it. She'd already posted it when I spoke to her last night,' said Bonita.

'There is no post delivery on Sundays,' said Parnold.

'She must have delivered it by hand then,' said Bonita.

'You got this today?' asked Campbell.

'I told you I did,' said Christine.

Parnold cautioned them and Campbell slipped the letter into his pocket so he could clip handcuffs on Christine. He wanted to ask her more about the night her father died. Her trail of lies and deceits gave her pale complexion a guilty look.

He realised what he'd missed last night when he'd been painting the spare room. He had noted the people involved but the connections had been wrong. Christine was really there with Kenneth Kran. A dangerous combination, thought Campbell. Surely, her lies had been to protect him, not her mother?

'What about Kinera Kran?' asked Parnold as he shut the back door of the car. The last of the two women were installed with Gowan in between looking glum.

'I don't think we can do anything about her right now. Sending a letter like this does not amount to inciting a riot. Even if we were to prove she sent it.'

Parnold took the driver's seat so Campbell made himself comfortable next to him. When Christine had calmed down he would question her again, but meanwhile he would take a rest. He stretched his legs as best he could and tried to relax knowing the tense, exacting environment of the police station was only twenty minutes away.

Chapter 15

The door squawked open and banged shut behind them. Stark paint shone too much light in his eyes while hard floor tiles seemed unforgiving to Campbell's hot feet. The high ceiling took every sound and made it harder and sharper. The smell of disinfectant filtered through the polish.

The duty officer took down the details from Parnold and told Campbell he was wanted by Chief Inspector Tarnish upstairs. Campbell started to frame the words to ask his sergeant to keep Christine Pleasance until he could speak to her, when Gowan said,

'Inspector, I think I should really stay with you. If I keep being sent off with other officers I don't get a true picture of your work.'

Campbell felt his sweaty back chill and he gripped the desk instead of Gowan's neck. He wanted to tell him he was being plain nosy and a lot more besides, instead he asked, 'Do you have a box to tick for a rollicking from the boss?' He turned and went through the security door to the offices. He heard Gowan follow him; his crepe soled shoes squeaking on the polished floor.

When they reached the boss's office Gowan was told by a growl from its six foot five occupant to wait outside. Chief Inspector Tarnish almost bowed as he saw Campbell into the seat opposite his own. Campbell wanted to ask him what he was doing in on a Sunday afternoon, but he kept his mouth closed.

Seated but not comfortable, Campbell watched Chief Inspector Tarnish lean back in his large padded chair and ask,

'What are you doing spending all this man-power chasing lorries?' The Chief Inspector's burnished baldhead remained smooth while his flattened features were levelled into a hard stare.

'We think they are dumping chemical waste, Sir,' said Campbell holding his pleasant, polite, co-operative look as best he could.

'That's the local council's responsibility or government agency, not ours. You are being scrutinised for your efficiency. Gowan's report is not just for my eyes. It will be looked at by others. You are investigating a murder.'

'Aye, Sir,' said Campbell falling back on his Scottishness for comfort. 'It's a possibility that someone who was dumping or connected with the dumping murdered Graham Pleasance. He was the council's waste officer. He acted outside his duties. So I want to catch whoever's doing it and question them.'

Tarnish swung forward, leaned across the desk and said, 'Make sure you do.' His vast hand left the desk top and opened a drawer. It returned with a memory stick. 'An anonymous phone call came in at ten-thirty this morning while you were out.'

Campbell placed that at about the time he opened Eira Dublin's fishing cottage door. He watched his senior officer place it into his computer. Tarnish pressed a few keys and a false squeaky voice gave details of a proposed dumping operation. Campbell pulled out his notebook from his pocket. He realised that he'd torn the fabric as well as a couple of pages of his notes in the scuffle with Bonita Arlotte and Christine Pleasance, so he turned to an unblemished page and jotted down the details.

'And I want the local council and government agency informed,' said Tarnish, squaring his already straight shoulders.

Campbell didn't feel inclined to argue. He'd heard the tale of how Tarnish, in his rugby playing days, had run the length of the pitch to punch another player out. Rumour had it that it was one of his own team.

Sighing Campbell tracked a spider across the sun-drenched dashboard. Of course Christine Pleasance, as well as Bonita Arlotte, had been released by the time he'd come out of the boss's office. Gowan's fault again, he assumed. At least no-one from the council or government agency had wanted to come with the surveillance team.

Parnold, under Campbell's directions, had parked behind the hedgerow in the lane beyond the Ouse Crossing site that had been mentioned on the tape. Campbell looked across the fields noting the sparse grass and yellow weeds rolling over the hilltop. The chalk ground structure formed convolutions which, below them, were covered by dark man-planted forestry. The dusty soil here was so different from the black fens of Sparrow Bank.

Campbell wasn't going to trust the information from the tip-off so he had a car in place ready to follow Kenneth Kran's lorries from their depot halfway between Sparrow Bank and Hillvill.

'Sunday nights should be a film and an Indian take-away,' said Parnold.

Campbell viewed the other cars supposedly hidden around the field and parked on the industrial estate behind. Garden and Jenner were parked in a gateway nearby. He could see them talking. He wondered if they were discussing a particular subject or just emptying themselves of the day's clutter. They caught his look and stopped. The evening moved on. The air cooled enough for him to reach for his jacket. He hadn't worn it since his interview with Chief Inspector Tarnish.

He couldn't complain, thought Campbell. He had managed to find someone on the end of the council's out of hour's number but he hadn't been keen to come out. Graham Pleasance hadn't been replaced yet and the man he spoke to was quite happy to prosecute for dumping on police evidence.

Night came only slowly. To Campbell the quiet became a nothingness. Suddenly he realised he couldn't define himself. He'd become so much part of the background he wouldn't be surprised if there was no record of his existence – until a message came through that one of Kran's lorries was on the move.

Parnold asked which direction. The reply came, 'Towards Hillvill.'

'Damn,' said Parnold.

'Hush,' said Campbell. 'That isn't quite the wrong direction. It can still take the Ouse Crossing road from there.' The ticking of his watch was only interrupted by the radio crackling briefly and a clipped Norfolk accent saying, 'He's at the Hillvill round-a-bout now,' and then, 'He's going north to Bishop's Town.'

Parnold swore while Campbell gave instructions to the shadow car to keep following.

Half an hour later they were informed the lorry had drawn into a park by the docks and had been locked and left there by the driver.

Parnold punched the dashboard.

Campbell exercised his ankles for a moment considering whether to disband their watch, until he heard the shriek of crashing lorry gears from the access road to the industrial estate. He looked up to see faces caught white by turning headlights. A small lorry pulled into the gateway. Through the thin hedge he saw the cab door open letting out the voice of a disk jockey and powerful music from the radio. The interior light flashed on showing a check-shirted man wearing a red baseball cap. Campbell watched him jump down and noted his shiny black wellingtons. The man slammed the door shut. A shadow moved on the far seat.

'There's someone in there with him,' whispered Parnold.

The driver was looking towards the cab. He stretched before putting on gloves and a white facemask, which he'd pulled out of his trouser pocket. Campbell recognised it as the sort of thing he used when he'd laid extra loft insulation last year.

'Amateurish,' said Parnold.

'It's more than we've got,' said Campbell. 'We haven't brought any protective clothing with us.' He paused wishing the man from the council had warned him. 'It seems pointless to watch the contamination of this field. We might as well act now.'

Parnold gave the signal and the occupants of the other cars rushed out. Campbell allowed the others to go ahead and assess the unfolding situation. He watched the baseball capped man spring round at the movement of the police officers. For a moment the lorry driver braced himself with his legs spread and knees bent and his hands held up in a ready-to-fight stance until more police came from the edges of the field and others jumped the wire fencing from the industrial site.

Parnold shouted, 'Police, stop!'

But the driver, still masked, turned and wrenched on the cab handle. He got the door open and was nearly in when a track-suited Jenner, the first to reach him, clutched his foot. Her blond ponytail caught the light from inside the cab. Garden was just behind her.

Because of the shadowy movement he'd seen in the passenger seat earlier Campbell said, 'Quick, the other side,' to Parnold as he came up. He heard his sergeant pass on this order to two other officers as he caught a glimpse inside the cab. Garden was hauling at the lorry driver's jeans. The policewomen, now helped by others, pulled him out of the cab. He landed in front of Campbell. Parnold moved forward to hold the man still.

All Campbell could see was the facemask and the tattered, red baseball cap as he ducked and weaved, so he plucked off the hat. In the dark his hair looked black. It fell forward only to be thrown back by its owner's defiant flick of the head. He'd hoped for fair to greying blond. But black hair meant nothing: a paid employee at best, knowing nothing of murder.

'The door's locked,' shouted one of the officers on the far side of the lorry.

'Just stay there,' yelled Parnold.

'Hell,' said Garden still half in the cab, her exit blocked by the tangle of officers around the lorry driver. Campbell moved to look inside. He heard a growl. Images of the Wet Goose pub yard, a black and tan dog, of being cornered by brick walls and of chocolate flitted through his mind.

'I haven't got my dog-scarer,' said Jenner.

So Campbell pressed the button on the one he'd picked up and kept with him since the incident in the pub yard.

The dog leapt over Garden and Jenner knocking into Parnold and the other policemen holding the black haired lorry driver. Stretching its long black legs the animal dodged the occasional policeman and headed for the gate.

Campbell could see the grip on the lorry driver was weakened and lunged at him. But he was too late; the black haired man slipped from their hands and ran, lifting his feet over the hard rough ground, in the same direction as his dog. Halfway to the gate he pulled off his facemask. By now everyone was giving chase. The lorry driver side-stepped a couple of policemen but he was losing ground to Parnold who was heading the pack. Campbell could see him because of his sergeant's height. He started to walk after them.

Parnold broke away from the others and dived at the lorry driver's legs. They tumbled together on the stony ground. When Campbell arrived Parnold was sitting on his catch, and he decided it would be best to leave them thus for the questioning process. He peered at the driver's dusty flabby face.

'It's Harry Sturning from the Wet Goose Pub, Sir,' said Jenner from beside him.

Campbell weighed the circumstances in his mind. Sturning hadn't actually got round to dumping any waste and the powers for dealing with the offence rested with the council anyway. None of his officers had been hurt – only given some exercise. He did not have the legal right to arrest him for dumping though he was sure he could think of something if he needed to. So he said, 'If you tell us what you know we won't need to take this any further.'

He saw Parnold wince at this unofficial-style of approach.

Harry Sturning said nothing.

'Do you realise the consequences of dumping chemical waste here?' asked Campbell.

'A few hundred quid,' said Sturning.

'The chemicals,' said Campbell, 'would run down through the sandy soil into the chalk layers and into the ground water which is used for the town's drinking supply.'

'He didn't tell me that,' said Sturning.

'Who?'

'It's my first time, honest.'

'Who?' repeated Campbell.

A car started in the lane. Campbell looked up. No one had been told to leave. He glanced over the people around him. No one had left. He and Parnold, Jenner and Garden had been the only ones parked out in the lane. He guessed that in the commotion the arrival of an on-looker had not been noticed. Yet, why go now? The truly curious were usually there until moved on. Campbell shook away his paranoia with a movement of his head and told himself it was a public road.

'Let me up and I'll tell you,' said Sturning.

Campbell looked at him and at Parnold. He couldn't be sure that his sergeant was not doing more than just keeping his prisoner from running away so he agreed.

Still firmly held, but now upright, he said, 'I didn't exactly lie when I said I didn't recognise Kenneth Kran. I hadn't met him until the night that Pleasance bloke went in the river. It was then that he said he could put a bit of work my way. Well, the pub doesn't pay so I agreed.'

'Kenneth Kran employed you to dump waste?'

'Yes.'

'The lorry to the docks was a decoy,' said Parnold.

'Lies and more lies,' said Jenner turning her face away.

'Where did the waste come from?' asked Campbell.

'I don't know,' said Harry Sturning. 'I collected the lorry from the farm next to the one where they're picking strawberries. Kran keeps some of his heavy machinery down there.'

Having watched Parnold empty Harry Sturning's pockets, like the good ratter he was, Campbell instructed Jenner and Garden to take another officer and escort Sturning home. He was allowed to take his house keys while the lorry keys and a small hunting knife in a leather pouch were kept back.

By the time he'd issued these instructions he was getting into the car. 'Parnold,' he said, 'Kenneth Kran's office. We'll start there. I expect he's waiting for a phone call from our publican friend at this very moment. If he's not there we can still take a look.' He rubbed the back of his neck. With Alec Gowan at home reading or tucked up in bed instead of standing behind him with his clipboard he'd been able to think clearly. Yes, it hadn't gone badly. Kenneth Kran was now the chief suspect for the murders of Sheena Kiljames and Graham Pleasance. His arrest tonight would surely solve these ugly crimes and protect Maggie Norrice.

Chapter 16

It would be her last visit to the Wet Goose Public House, decided Kinera. Twice now she'd been seen returning. The first time it had been her ex-husband and Christine Pleasance, the night Graham pleasance died. The funny thing was that with all the excitement of the car in the river the stupid publicans hadn't seemed to've noticed they'd been broken into. And then the other night that hateful cat woman, Maggie Norrice, had seen her – her and her blasted night-time walks.

Kinera Kran stood and looked at the sleeping children. She'd been denied this pleasure from her own son, now she had to steal it from common people such as these. It didn't seem fair.

Tonight it'd been easier to get in. There hadn't been any dog to drug and the new locks on the doors were pointless when she could jump on the flat roof of the toilet block from the riverbank and climb through one of the first floor windows. The bathroom casement was particularly rotten and easily forced. She half wondered about collecting some more gin from the bar but decided against it. Tonight she would just look at the children. She didn't mean them any harm. They couldn't help their parentage any more than she could help drinking alcohol. All the times she'd broken in she'd never even touched them.

The nearly full moon lit the thin curtain and shone on the children's smooth faces, black hair and dark still lashes. Their calm eased her for a moment as it always did. Her own child had slept like this. How she craved to have him back – un-dead – running, laughing, funny, curiously perceptive, unable to contain his energy, sometimes violent. His wickedness had caused her to consider the religious concept of 'original sin'. Were people born with evil in their souls? If so surely it couldn't be got rid of by water and prayer, only adopted by a religion?

What sin could these sleeping children contain, waiting and festering until it was given the chance to burst forth in adulthood? She hoped they wouldn't be like Kenneth, her once-upon-a-time husband. A lust for money had been his sin. And she still kept his name, because it had been her son's. Every time she painted she was seduced by the dark green shadows, purples, crimsons on her canvas. Her grief became great sweeps of colour shaping items of beauty into the forms of nightmare. Her paintings were like the blood from her veins, the water from the river. They were everything.

They were all that was left of her. She didn't live outside them. Her son was gone. She had a Spanish stranger in her house – but she would soon leave. Kinera wondered briefly how Christine Pleasance had reacted to her letter about Kenneth and Bonita. She'd delivered it this morning. She knew where she lived. She'd followed Kenneth one day there. And, she hadn't been home since – too busy.

She smiled. A child stirred. Kinera looked to leave. She would not come again. There would be no need.

A car was coming from the north, she could hear it across the fen. Any noise late at night would disturb this village. She made for the bathroom window. By the time she reached it the car had pulled in the pub yard. She guessed it would be at the front and out of view of the flat roof but its occupants would be able to see her escape route across the riverbank.

Closing the window from the outside a movement on the bank caught her attention. She flung herself flat on the roof. The small black grains of gravel ground into her skin. It was that Norrice woman out on the riverbank with that nosy post woman, Sparrow. Had that ridiculous, fat, letter reading cow taken to night prowling with her relation? The police had done nothing about them despite her note. How she hated them.

Her chest felt tight and she wished for her thermal flask discretely filled with gin. She wondered if Maggie Norrice and the post woman had seen her. Not wanting to look down competed with a desire to see the faces of the people speaking in the pub yard. She decided she couldn't see without the hazy moonlight catching her pale skin so she lay flatter and hid her face. The voice of a man, a woman and another man came up to her on the sultry night air. She only recognised the one belonging to the landlord.

Keys jangled, locks clicked, gravel twisted under feet, car doors slammed, an engine started and wheels rolled away.

When she looked up she saw Maggie Norrice and the post woman on the riverbank watching the car go back over the bridge and head north out of Sparrow Bank. They walked back over the bank and up to the bridge. Maggie Norrice was always seeing things she shouldn't. Well, she wouldn't be doing any more snooping soon. She had other plans for her.

Behind Kinera the bathroom light came on so she jumped onto the riverbank and squatted there waiting for the women on the bridge to go. She thought she saw Maggie Norrice look round at her, but she could not be sure.

In the Wet Goose the bathroom window was being opened. The beam of light from it splayed over the flat roof, the kitchen and barn into a garden beyond catching a climbing frame and swings, a white plastic table and chairs. But it didn't reach Kinera on the bank. The window slammed shut. Maggie Norrice and the post woman were gone. She expected to get home without any more trouble.

Campbell called, 'Mr Kran, Police,' as he watched Parnold turn the handle of the flimsy portable-office door. The light from its window fell on the fair jaw of his sergeant and he wondered if his expression was one of extreme concentration or anger. Car doors behind him slammed as other policemen joined them in the yard.

The door opened. Campbell called again and waited for a moment on the doormat. He heard a movement beyond the dimpled glass reception screen so he went through to the office.

'Mr Kran,' he called.

'In here,' came the shout of a familiar voice, but it wasn't the tight Oxbridge accents of Kenneth Kran. The voice was Irish.

On entering the small office Campbell could see why. Kenneth Kran lay face down on the ribbed carpet tiles, a couple of which – one by his mouth, another by his hand – were whitened. And Eira Dublin stood over him.

'Thank God you're here,' said Eira.

'Is he alive?' asked Campbell.

'I think he might be. When I came in I thought he was choking on his bonds. He was tied around his neck to his chair so I cut the cords with my penknife and he fell to the floor.'

'Parnold. Ambulance. And get a first aider in here,' shouted Campbell.

'What have you touched, Mr Dublin?' Campbell looked at the cup and saucer on the stained carpet.

'Just the nylon cords and the door. Perhaps the chair.'

Campbell placed his hands in his pockets and followed Dublin's route across the office. He viewed Kenneth Kran. He could smell chlorine and, looking at the corner of Kran's face, he could see where chemical burns had corroded the skin inside and around his mouth. Cut cords lay about his neck, hands and feet. The flesh was gauged around his wrists and throat. He reached out and touched him. There was a distant pulse.

Campbell sat next to Dublin in the back of the car while the ambulance rolled into the yard. He watched its crew stretcher Kenneth Kran into its brightly-lit interior and take him away to hospital. Forensic would be along later. He hoped the evidence they would collect would not be needed to find another murderer, just Kenneth's attacker.

However, the chance to question Dublin without Alec Gowan looking over his shoulder and ticking boxes was delightful. He realised the long night had made him light headed. To sober himself he looked at the Irishman's hands. They were trembling.

'I thought I was going to kill Kenneth Kran until I saw him like that,' said Eira Dublin. It was almost an Irish lament. 'I knew he must've killed Graham Pleasance. But he didn't have to kill Sheena. I wish he'd killed me instead. I knew what he was up to as much as they did.'

'And what was that?' Campbell glanced at Parnold pacing the short distance between Kran's office and the car, and back again like a horse with a nervous twitch.

'Wanton pollution.' Eira took a deep breath. 'I knew that the land I'd bought was used for agriculture before it was given planning permission as an industrial site so when Sheena...' His voice failed for a second. 'So when Sheena suggested having a soil sample done before I purchased it I nearly said, 'No'. Samples were taken and the results came back clean as a blue sky in Tipperary.'

'A lack of rain in those parts is quite rare, I understand.'

Eira stopped shaking. He nearly smiled. 'Later I brought in construction engineers to survey the site. They complained about a strange smell and insisted I had some soil samples done. I told them I already knew the site to be clear, but it made no difference. When I got the report and it was contaminated with all the filth I told you about earlier. I couldn't believe it. I told them so.'

'So someone was dumping, how did you know it was Kenneth Kran?'

'I didn't at first. I even got him to quote me for cleaning up the site. Then I told Sheena what had happened. She showed me a list of vehicle numbers Graham Pleasance suspected of dumping. She knew they were numbers from my lorries. I'd reported them stolen by that time. I think Sheena suspected me for a while. Perhaps that's why she got me to take that first soil test. I often wonder if she'd been watching me the day we met. But why would I pollute my own land?'

'For a quick profit. People still pay to get rid of difficult stuff.' Campbell turned to look squarely at Dublin.

'And the business would get prosecuted for not using a licensed waste contractor as well as the dumper, in your scenario myself. My business is food, Inspector, not toxic waste disposal.'

Campbell looked at his own hands – bony long fingers, straight and steady. 'It looks to me as if Kenneth Kran was poisoned, Mr Dublin.'

'I was trying to save him.'

'So why hadn't you phoned for an ambulance?'

'I hadn't time.'

'We've only got your word for that.'

'Sheena.' The Irishman made it sound like, 'Think what you want,' and wiped his eyes with his fist.

The air in the car was stifling. Campbell opened the window next to him. 'It's all too late for keeping quiet. Sheena Kiljames is no longer your secret. She's dead and it looks very much as though Kenneth Kran murdered her. You wanted to kill him. You said so. And you were standing over him when I arrived. So I need to know it all, Mr Dublin.'

Eira Dublin looked down. 'Graham, Sheena and I took turns to watch Kenneth Kran's yard. Graham suspected him from the start. Then, by chance, we got a break through. We found he had some lorries and other equipment hidden at a farm a bit out of Sparrow Bank.'

'Drain farm?' asked Campbell, remembering what Harry Sturning from the pub had said about getting the dumping lorry from a farm in that direction.

'No, the one next to it. Graham and Sheena spotted him while taking soil samples at Drain Farm.' Eira Dublin leaned over and covered his face with his hands. He mumbled, 'Then Graham was killed.'

Campbell said, 'If you'd told us this earlier Sheena might not have died.'

'I didn't know where she was. I thought telling you would put her in danger. I didn't know what to do.'

'Tell me what happened tonight.'

Eira pulled himself upright, 'Tonight I followed the lorry and saw it draw into that field at Ouse Crossing. I saw you lot there. I had my proof at last. I came back here to have it out with him. And he was… Well, you saw.'

He sounded genuine enough to Campbell, and Eira Dublin had seemed relieved to see him when he'd arrived in Kenneth Kran's office. So he asked, 'Have you any evidence of your actions?'

'We kept a log on loose sheets, which we filed. There are photographs of the lorries at the farm at Sparrow Bank. They're at my office.'

"Och well," thought Campbell. "It seems to tie in with Sturning's story." He would get Jenner to go and check the papers. She was already on her way here from the station where the officers had returned following the lorry watch.

'His own daughter secured Graham's death, and Sheena's,' said Dublin looking straight at Campbell.

Campbell noted a desperate honesty in his blue eyes. 'Oh?' he asked.

'It had to be Christine ruddy Pleasance passing on information from her father's investigations. I saw her and Kenneth Kran together a month ago. I couldn't bring myself to tell Graham.'

'Thank you, Mr Dublin,' said Campbell getting out of the car. 'Stay there, will you? One of my officers will take you for fingerprinting.'

From the events related to him he found it unsurprising that Kenneth Kran had been poisoned. He squashed the feeling that some sort of justice might have been done, because it was for him to catch the criminals and bring them to trial. That was the only way justice could be seen to be done. The poisoner was now outside the law. And, in turn, Campbell had to hunt and catch that person to answer for this crime. He flexed his tired shoulders.

Kenneth Kran was certainly unable to tell him anything about his attacker, and, no doubt, he would be in that condition for some time, if he survived. A bedside vigil was required. After all, Kenneth Kran had a lot of questions to answer himself. He called to Parnold, who was just about to drive Eira Dublin to the Ouse Crossing police station, and instructed him to organise the hospital watch.

So, if Eira Dublin was genuine – and he felt he was – it seemed likely that one other human being with as much reason to have a heart full of revenge was Christine Pleasance.

But his train of thought was interrupted by cars swinging in front of him, throwing dust up into the warm air. Blue lights flicked colouring the yard. Among others, WDC Jenner and WPC Garden got out of one of the vehicles, while Alec Gowan appeared from the rear of another. Campbell wondered how many boxes he could tick between here and Christine's home in Cambridge.

Chapter 17

Janet Sparrow had started to clean the tiny living room of Pump Cottage by the light of the bare electric bulb when she and Auntie Maggie had returned from their walk along the bank. Dust was like the past, as far as she was concerned, best cleaned away. Daylight broke through the gap in the grubby curtains making the dust in the air dance.

As she made her plump arms brush and scrub she blamed herself, her parents, the village and then the River Sparrow for causing Aunt Maggie's misery. She watched the dust collect again on the cleaned surface. At least it was something to do now that Auntie slept.

For someone who'd always found sleep easy and enjoyable she found it strange that she should be the one to keep watch over the old woman. Yet tonight the uneasiness she'd felt for Aunt Maggie's safety was worse than ever. Suppose her son, Matthew, was the murderer and it wasn't just someone who looked like her husband from all those years ago? Even if the man on the bridge wasn't her son, couldn't he come back to silence her anyway?

She finished with the mantelpiece and the telly in the corner she'd given Aunt Maggie and went over to deal with the dining table. It was while she was rubbing polish into the marked wood that she found the drawer underneath intended for cutlery and linen. A paper poked out of the corner of it. Janet opened the drawer to straighten the contents and noticed a scrapbook on top of the wayward sheet. She took it out and opened it on the newly polished table-top.

It was full of newspaper clippings: stiff and brittle, yellowed, wrinkled by glue. There were pictures of skaters and cups from the nineteen-twenties. She knew her aunt was still trapped in her past by the loss of

Matthew. Yet, she shared the present with her and even that was now tangled with the past.

The sky turned a hazy lemon colour as the sun rose higher above the fenland sky, and birds in the hedge twittered noisily.

As she put the book back she went to straighten the sheet that had caused her to open the drawer in the first place. The handwriting on the paper caught her attention. She looked again. She knew it was Kinera Kran's. Having read it she said, 'That woman makes my blood boil.' But she didn't have time for anger, it was getting late. She checked her watch. It was time to collect the post.

Janet could see Bonita Arlotte standing outside Kinera Kran's house from the bridge. Her long black hair was caught back and tied with a scarf, and her long legs were covered by a flimsy cotton skirt. Suitcases and art folders were strung out along the roadside. The first American aeroplane of the day jetted overhead on its way to the bombing range on the Wash.

When Janet approached Bonita said, 'I cannot wait in there.' She nodded behind her. 'In her house.'

'Is anyone in?' asked Janet propping her bike laden with the village's post against the hedge. She wanted to face Kinera Kran about those notes.

'I don't know. I don't think so. I say nothing, I just leave.'

Janet wiped her brow. Her body's sweat couldn't escape into the already humid air.

'Kinera, she's crazy,' said Bonita distracted by a vehicle approaching along the fen road. 'Ah, taxi.'

Flexing her thick legs in readiness to help with the baggage, Janet knew that Bonita would ordinarily ignore her. It was only because there was no one else around she even spoke. And it wasn't really to her. She seemed to be talking to some invisible person just above and behind her.

An oldish blue saloon with a white plastic moulding on the roof, announcing the taxi's phone number, drew up alongside.

'I ought to charge you double for the damage that road's done to my car,' the driver complained.

It wasn't so much that she was pleased the Spanish girl was going, it was more the habit of helping that made her hand bags and folders to the driver.

Bonita Hugged and kissed Janet. It seemed strange, as she'd not even passed the time of day with her since her arrival nearly three months ago.

When the taxi'd taken Bonita back over the bridge towards the railway station, a good eight miles away, Janet turned with her letter back to Kinera's door. As she pushed it through the letterbox the door swung open.

'Silly girl,' said Janet, 'didn't shut the door properly.' She went to close it but she changed her mind. OK so Kinera wasn't there to confront about the notes she'd been sending to Aunt Maggie, but she could find out about the woman who'd sent them. For a moment she thought about going over the threshold of right and wrong, of stepping uninvited into someone else's privacy. And then she fell back into the childhood curiosity that had taken her into Auntie Maggie's house when she was eleven years old. She knew this strange woman was up to something and it had something to do with all those letters she sent and received.

Beyond the living room was a door to the staircase. The narrow stairs creaked under her weight. She would start at the top in the attic studio with its huge window staring out across the river: the room was full of paintings: a frozen river; red tulips under a black sky; a daffodil field with craters in it, the yellow flowers crushed around their edges. She didn't understand this woman's paintings that turned beautiful things into ugliness. And there was no typewriter or similar device, nor were there any letters to be seen. She trembled as she came out.

Down from there she found a small bedroom. The white cupboards were bare. A white telephone sat on the bedside table. The only colour in the room came from a patterned shawl lying on the floor. Janet remembered it as one Bonita had worn around her waist on the strawberry field at Drain farm.

The other room was brown with dark-stained wood furniture. A bureau stood between a blanket box and a dressing table smudged with lipstick and powder. She opened the lid. A laptop stood on the writing desk. She pushed her hands into the cubby-holes behind and pulled out bundles of papers: bills and receipts but no letters. There was nothing like the smart white envelopes she'd delivered almost daily to this address.

She sat on the rucked up pile of quilt left in a heap on the bed. As she put her hand down she felt silk. She pulled it back and saw she'd touched Kinera's underwear. She leapt up, no longer wanting to be in this private place. She ran down the stairs and into the living room. It was the only way out of the house. On reaching the door she looked back and saw the wooden box by the window, a glass carafe holding a clear liquid on top, an empty glass next to that.

Janet went over to the glass and sniffed it. Gin. 'Kinera wrote her notes when she was drunk,' she said out loud. Some instinct made her pull the carafe and glass from the lid and open the box. Bundles of letters neatly tied with string lined the bottom of it.

A few letters lay on top, unbound. Flicking through she realised many were stamped with the brand names of manufacturers. Yes, these were the ones she was after. It seemed odd she hadn't realised before that nearly all the letters she'd brought to this address had been like this. Janet's plump, hot fingers seemed to stick to the paper as she tried to open them.

She read a couple. They were apologies for complaints Kinera'd made about food she'd bought and copies of her letters of complaint. One mentioned that her child had nearly choked on a piece of metal found in a tin of peas – it was dated just a year ago. Another complained about an acid taste in the food.

'What child?' she asked herself. Another American jet passed overhead. It was flying low and the shriek of its engines forced her to drop her letters and cover her ears. The plane passed over and another pain, this time in the back of her head, took away her consciousness.

Chapter 18

Campbell rubbed sleep out of his eyes. He'd used the journey across the southern fens to Cambridge for some much-needed sleep. He hadn't dreamed, but when he woke he remembered his earlier nightmare of being under water and still being alive. It made him wonder if Kenneth Kran was still surviving.

Alec Gowan was behind Campbell, following him up the half dozen stone front steps to the main entrance of the flats where Christine Pleasance lived. He could almost feel the man's excitement through his back.

While Parnold went around the rear of the building with one of the local police force, WPC Garden and another local policeman joined Campbell and Gowan under the front porch. Campbell pressed the second button of the row of five by the door. It was labelled "Ms Pleasance". There was no answer. Campbell started to rock back on his heels and forwards onto his toes.

He was stopped by a female shout tearing at the air around him. This was followed by heavy steps travelling quickly from somewhere above, through an echoing hall and then down some stairs towards them. She was still shouting when she flung open the front door and then she stopped. He could see it wasn't Christine. This girl's eighteen-year-old, unblemished face was distorted with temper.

'What do you want?' asked the girl, clad in cut-down jeans and tee-shirt.

'We're here to see Christine Pleasance,' said Campbell showing her his identity.

'Good. Then you can get her out of the blasted bathroom. We have to share.'

As Campbell made for the stairs he heard the girl say sarcastically, 'Help yourself, I would.'

He was half way up when he was joined by Parnold and the other local policeman, who'd gone round to cover the back door, before he reached the first floor bathroom.

Campbell called at the door. When there was no reply he asked WPC Garden to be ready to go in with him. Bracing himself Campbell opened the door and placed his hands in his pockets. Blood from Christine's slashed wrists mingled with water. The large bath's big tap dripped spreading a ripple over her feet and legs. These were loose – supported by water, not life. In her nakedness her femininity was obvious and her light brown hair was no longer tied back. It floated in the juices that had made it grow, framing her square jaw and strong cheekbones.

From behind Campbell heard WPC Garden back off and Alec Gowan fall against the landing wall dropping his clipboard. Campbell moved forward a couple of paces away from the efficiency expert, being helped down the stairs by Garden, and sniffed at a glass standing on a stool beside the bath. Whiskey.

'Alcohol,' said Campbell. 'The forever sedative.'

In her room along the landing Campbell found notes about Kenneth Kran's lorries made by Christine's father on the table. He recognised the neat square writing even with the word, 'No' scrawled over each page in red ink. He read the information and found it agreed with Eira Dublin's story. He showed it to Parnold who'd followed him into the room.

'Graham Pleasance never told his daughter about Kenneth Kran's dumping operation,' said Campbell. 'She must've seen these papers when she was going through his things following his death. And it must've been after she found the lorry numbers and given them to us.' Campbell waved the papers at Parnold. 'Without the rest of her father's notes she wouldn't have realised their importance to Kenneth Kran. She may even have known that those numbers didn't belong to Kran's lorries so she might have thought they may even keep us away from her lover.'

'She wouldn't have shown them if she'd known Kran'd nicked the number plates,' agreed Parnold.

'She wasn't exactly an innocent,' said Campbell, nodding at is colleague.

'She must have told Kenneth Kran about her father's movements,' said Parnold. 'I expect it was his trip to Drain Farm, so close to his other vehicles that ensured his fate. She must have lied to us about not knowing about her father's involvement in soil sampling, especially as she made that approach to Sheena Kiljames. When she realised all this from these papers she must've gone to look for Sheena to warn her. She only found her when we did, already dead.'

Campbell ran his gaze over the vast marble mantelpiece. He avoided the cold surface as he retrieved a fold of paper tucked behind the carriage clock in the centre.

'I've organised the team, Sir,' said Parnold.

Unfolding the note, Campbell saw that it was addressed to him. Underneath the day's date and the time of noon, which was two hours ago, it read:

'I'm sorry for what I've done. Please don't tell my mother about my involvement with Kenneth Kran. I know now he killed my father. I hope my tip-off last night stopped the contamination of more land.

'I did it for my dad. And it is not enough to balance the wickedness I have done to him and Sheena, and my mother. As you'll have to see her to tell her about my death please say goodbye for me,

Christine Pleasance.'

Campbell looked out of the window at Gowan sitting in the police car with the door open and his feet on the kerb. His head was between his knees. If only he hadn't distracted him in the police station after Christine's arrest he might've been able to talk to her: find out all this; prevent her suicide.

'That's that then, Sir,' said Parnold with the breathless satisfaction of a Grand National winner. 'We can pack up and go home. Kenneth Kran murdered Graham Pleasance and Sheena Kiljames and, once she realised what was going on, Christine tried to kill Kenneth Kran and then had a go at herself.'

'We will have to see what Kenneth Kran has to say when he's fit enough. But it certainly looks that way at the moment,' agreed Campbell.

'Just think,' said Parnold, 'how she's saved tax payers' money: no time gobbling arrests, interviews or trials – very tidy and efficient.'

Inspecting his jacket pocket, which had been torn during Christine's fight with Bonita on the riverbank, Campbell said, 'We are not here to save the tax payers' money. We are here to solve crimes, to maintain law and order and bring suspects forward for justice to be done.' He turned away from the window overcome for a moment by the fact that the death toll in this investigation had suddenly become three, and possibly four if Kenneth Kran died. 'Fenland water,' he muttered. Ignoring Parnold's glance meaning, "He's off again", and went back to the bathroom door.

He watched the cool dark pink mixture lapping around Christine. This water had never reached the Wash. It had been taken from the river on its way there. It had been cleaned and sent along a network of pipes to this suicide. This bath was a sluice gate in its life – and it stopped Campbell as it stopped the course of the river. If the plug was pulled the water would drain away to be cleaned and returned to the river to continue its journey out to the fen's basin. But his own energy had been taken from him. This death and Kran's torture had happened because he'd been distracted by Alec Gowan. Efficiency. For him the sluice gate was locked: the guilt of Kenneth Kran and Christine could not be tested until Kenneth Kran recovered.

He corrected himself: Alec Gowan was not a murderer.

Campbell spotted WPC Garden sitting on the wall outside examining her shoes. Her hat was pushed back and a fluffy wedge of hair had fallen forward over her eyes. He joined her, concerned that the bathroom upstairs had started to upset her now events were calming down.

'It doesn't matter,' he said, 'how often I see or smell blood it always feels like the first time.' His Edinburgh accent softened his words. And he recalled how Garden always seemed to link herself to the relatives or the person who'd found the body when called out to a crime. This he realised took her away from bloodshed.

'I'm alright, thanks.'

'It seems,' said Campbell, 'That humanity can only just keep its blood lust under control. Horror films and books satisfy that urge but the real thing is nauseating.'

'I find dreams help – even nightmares,' said Garden looking at him. She reminded Campbell of his daughter, Victoria, with her dark brown eyes and smooth, soft, almost sallow, complexion.

With her he watched the black plastic body bag being brought through the pillared porch and down the front steps.

'I write mine down,' she went on. 'But I don't dream of blood and gore like this. My dreams are in code. For instance, blood might be red fabric. I read them through until I work out what they mean.'

'I think of my dreams,' said Campbell, 'as a filing system sorting out the information I've gathered through the day.'

'Same sort of thing really,' said Garden leaning back slightly and swinging her legs out from the wall. Campbell thought she looked like a schoolgirl in the wrong uniform.

'But I've been dreaming of drowning,' he said. 'And it doesn't seem to sort anything.'

'Surely that's not surprising considering.'

'The thing is,' Campbell continued, 'it's me and I'm not drowning. I'm under water looking up and I can see the surface. I can't reach the air and I'm panicking but I know I'm able to live – I can still breath.'

Garden sucked her bottom lip for a moment before saying, 'It means you can cope. Events are trying to drown you, but you can still breath so that means you can handle them.'

'Thank you, Constable,' he said. Though he wondered: if he was sorting matters out, shouldn't he be swimming to the top of the water – not breathing underneath? He got up to leave; she looked a lot brighter.

'Thank you, Inspector,' said Garden standing up and straightening her uniform.

Maggie Norrice covered her grey matted hair with an old straw hat and changed her holed pink cardigan for a slightly less tatty one. It was going to be the last of the hot days today, she was sure.

She spat on a small mirror she'd found at the back of a shelf in the scullery and rubbed it with her sleeve. Unused to the glassy reflection of herself, she played with the mirror catching the sunlight and angling it across the room. It caught her dining table.

'Naughty Janet,' said Maggie to herself. Her voice softened and her fenland accent broadened, as if she were talking to a child. 'She's bin in my drawer.' She slipped out the scrap-book pushing back Kinera's crumpled notes, and opened it. There he was: her father moving over the solid ice – scratching, but not penetrating its cold perfection with his skates. It remained as unchanged as her past. She felt more like a child gazing into a frozen puddle, but unlike most children she was unable to stamp on that ice. She couldn't shatter the past, because from that past came Matthew. And Matthew had been here in Sparrow Bank, she'd seen him herself with her very own eyes. She was sure of that now.

Having shoved the book back in the drawer under the table she went to the door. She couldn't actually remember the last time she'd been up to the village during the daytime. Her husband had said nothing here was like his old life, or as good. He'd told her he really wanted to be in London, Birmingham or Leeds. But when he'd lived with her they'd gone nowhere. She used to go to Hillvill or Ouse Crossing occasionally before her mother died. Her father had stopped that with a, 'What do you want to go there for?' when she asked him for the bus fare.

Out in her lane, in front of the riverbank, the sun had turned hazy but it still made her blink. She thought of her cats sleeping on her bed unused to such daytime activity. Maggie reached the Wet Goose Public House. Its windows and doors were shut, the place still asleep. On the bridge she looked down at the River Sparrow. The water was high despite the recent dry spell. The wet spring had seen to that. A pair of swans with cygnets floated by and she was pleased her attempt to kill herself had failed.

'It's the mugginess that makes the river yellow,' she thought. 'And the water takes its colour from the sky.' She looked up to check her theory and remembered seeing Matthew's face caught in the pub's security light. If the boy's father had taken him, wouldn't he have brought him up to be like himself – cruel, selfish, violent? In that case he could have murdered that man in the car that night. And hadn't she seen him again, by Kinera's house?

The police were wrong. Janet was wrong. It hadn't been someone who looked like her husband, it had been her son Matthew. She'd been right on Saturday night. She had betrayed him. Janet's talk had persuaded her otherwise for a short while, but now she was certain. She had to warn him that the police were after him. She could forgive him anything. He was her son. If only he could forgive her. Even if he were to kill her she could accept that. She wasn't afraid.

'Kinera's house,' she said out loud. 'That's the last place I saw him, so that'll be the first place to try.'

The bridge seemed higher in the heat of the day. As she climbed she saw the chimney of the little cottage on the far side, then the roof, then the first floor windows, then the hawthorn hedge and then into the garden. And there she saw her son.

'Matthew,' she called.

Chapter 19

He said his name wasn't Matthew Norrice. He said it was Eira Dublin. Maggie took off her cardigan and laid it on the doorstep next to her son. She never expected him to have an Irish accent. But he'd been snatched from her so long ago and Jon could've taken him anywhere – why not Ireland? What else could've brought him across the Irish Sea, across England to the fens but the pull of blood ties?

The fact that he hadn't accepted her as his mother didn't worry her. He was so much like his father and he seemed to be the right age – there could be no mistake. And John was bound to have told him lies about his past.

Having listened to her story her son smiled and said, 'Not me, Missus. I'm as Irish as they come. I couldn't be related to you. And, please, call me Eira.'

'That's not important now, son,' said Maggie. 'I told the police I saw you the night the car went into the river and again a couple of nights later near Kinera Kran's house.'

He didn't seem to be listening but he said, 'The police know all about me, Mrs Norrice.'

'You must run away. Don't you see, I betrayed you.'

Her son touched her shoulder, 'You've betrayed no one. You told them what you saw, that's all.'

She soaked up his kindness. It warmed her better than the sun. Perhaps she'd been wrong about Jon teaching her boy cruelty; or it might be that Ireland had made him this way. She'd seen it on her telly: soft rolling hills and lush grass. She watched the man next to her. Could Jon Norrice bring up a child to be as gentle as this, even in Ireland?

Dust blew up along the River Authority roadway as a small-engined car roared towards them. Maggie heard it stop by the yellow metal gate that closed the lane to traffic. She wondered how the driver had got the car down there – the gate was always locked. Clogs rattling on the tarmac road stopped her. Then she saw a patterned scarf roped around chestnut and grey hair skimming along the top of the hedge. At the gateway she saw Kinera Kran.

She was only feet from her. She'd never been this close to her without a door between them. Kinera's face moved through different shades of mood from dark disgust, to a grey pleasure and then to a pale relief. Maggie frowned.

'Don't hiv nothin' to do with her, son,' she said grabbing his arm as he got up. She clung to him making her straw-hat fall off and she went with him to the gate.

She tugged at his shirt sleeve as Eira chuckled and said, 'Can I help you, Mrs Kran?'

Still clutching him she said, 'She sends notes.'

'I know,' said Eira. 'And you've not spoken to anyone for years, Mrs Norrice.'

'Thank goodness I've found someone,' said Kinera. 'There's a boy in the river. I can't swim. Bring a rope.'

'Have you called the police,' asked Eira Dublin.

'I just got through on my mobile phone before it went dead. They'll never get here in time. Hurry.'

Eira went to collect a rope while Maggie got her cardigan and followed Kinera back to the car. She left the straw hat where it was.

Did this peculiar neighbour from across the river know her past, Maggie wondered. Would she, of all people, give her a chance to balance the wrongs she'd committed so many years ago? She followed Kinera and Eira over the yellow gate. As the car had no rear passenger doors she got herself into the back seat through the gap made by Kinera pulling her seat forward. Sitting down she muttered to herself, 'Please, river, don't take another life.'

'Did you say something?' asked Kinera. Maggie watched her snap the driver's seat back in position and sit in it.

'No,' said Maggie. The car made her nervous. She'd been on busses but she couldn't remember ever being in a car before.

It rocked as Eira's bulk swung into the front passenger seat and placed the rope on his lap. Before he'd shut the door Kinera'd moved off.

'Eira Dublin's my son,' said Maggie. 'I haven't seen him since he was a baby and now I've found him after all this time.' She hadn't meant to say anything but it made her so happy.

'Really,' said Kinera to her. Maggie noted how she addressed Eira when she said, 'The boy's down here where I've been painting.'

Maggie felt sticky and hot. The air seemed impossible to breathe inside the car. She felt closed in by its metal sides and Eira's and Kinera's bulk in front of her. She tried to peek through the gap between their bodies but the rough lane shook her. She wondered what a real mobile phone would look like. Kinera'd said she had one. Maggie'd seen them on the telly. But she couldn't see one here. She supposed she must have left it on the riverbank.

The lurching and jarring turned the tightness in her gut to nausea. The bank made a green wall outside the left-hand window while the fields of unripe wheat beyond the ditch spread into a house-less distance through the right-hand window. They were going much further than she expected.

They'd gone past the bend in the river. If the boy were this far down surely the sluice keeper's house would have been nearer than Eira Dublin's? The keeper's cottage was the other side of the river but Kinera could have reached it by crossing the walkway on the sluice. P'raps he'd bin out.

At the base of the bank next to the sluice Kinera Kran said, 'We're here.' She jumped out of the car slamming the door. Eira followed. It was as if they'd forgotten her. But the life of the child was more important so she would find her way out of this car-trap. And she started to pull and push at the seats in front of her.

Campbell was still blaming Alec Gowan for Christine's death. He knew it was wrong to but that didn't seem to change the way he felt. Even having his nightmare analysed by Garden hadn't been able to take that away. The trip back to Cambridge seemed to have taken even longer than it had to get there. He knew it was because his rage was gnawing at his insides. He could feel the presence of the efficiency expert sitting behind him in the car. He could contain his anger no longer. He twisted round in his seat only to be aggravated more by not being able to see Gowan properly as he was tucked behind him. Instead he had a full view of WPC Garden blushing.

'She needn't have died,' he said squeezing out his Edinburgh accent through clenched teeth. He felt Parnold look at him. He read the emptiness of loss on his sergeant's face. Graham Pleasance had been his colleague and Christine had been Graham's daughter. Campbell understood Parnold's emptiness and feeling of uselessness – he felt the same way. 'If she'd spoken to someone she might have seen things differently,' he continued.

'I am only an observer,' said Alec Gowan. 'You shouldn't feel threatened or distracted by me. I am not here to upset your judgement. I will make my observations and make recommendations to improve work systems once I have gathered all the data.'

'By being here you imply criticism of our work,' snarled Campbell. 'You can go and tell Tarnish himself I'm not having you tailing me anymore. He can do what he likes, I've had enough.' He closed his mouth and turned back to the front. He wouldn't usually have said anything. He was almost ashamed of his outburst. He knew it had come from tiredness and frustration at the unhappy completion of this cycle of death.

The rest of the journey back to Norfolk was made in silence while Campbell picked at the dried paint on his hand. When they drew up into the slot in the police station car park, Parnold, Gowan and Garden made directly for the office. Campbell stayed next to the car looking at the bleak, flat, yellow bricked rear of the building. It made him feel deeply lonely. He wanted to be back home with his family, in his cottage. He wanted to be gloss painting the woodwork in his spare bedroom. He enjoyed the physical skill needed to produce a perfect finish.

He leaned on the car putting off the moment when he'd have to face Tarnish about his outburst to Alec Gowan. He had no doubt that right now the efficiency expert was telling all to the massive bundle of taut violence, which occupied the office at the top of the stairs.

The sky started to turn almost green above him and the air thickened until it tasted like rotten fruit. He saw WDC Jenner's blond head poke out of the rear door, see him, move effortlessly down the back steps and breeze over.

'Eira Dublin's papers panned out,' she said.

'Aye.'

'It's all over then, according to Sergeant Parnold, Sir.'

'Perhaps,' said Campbell wondering if she meant he might as well expect to lose his job through his lack of efficiency. No doubt his inability to save life because he was easily distracted by people with clipboards would be highlighted in Gowan's report.

'We'd better go and see Christine's mother,' said Jenner.

Campbell coughed. He hated this job. He let her drive, he knew she preferred to. He could never concentrate on the task of getting from A to B. There always seemed more important things to think about. This time he would reread the note Christine had left. The weight of his head leaning on his hand made his wrist ache. He didn't feel able to give support to anybody, let alone this poor woman who, in a matter of days, had lost both of her next of kin.

Jenner had been calm and strong while Campbell'd made every effort to gentle the woman's shock. Eventually they'd been able to retreat from the vacuum of emotion left by the news of Christine's death when a neighbour came round to help. No doubt, thought Campbell, Ruth Pleasance's brain was protecting her by not taking in the horror.

The outside air didn't refresh him. The sunlight that had lasted for weeks was darkened by heavy mauve clouds. Their arrival seemed strange to him, as he could feel no breeze.

'I don't think Christine tried to kill Kenneth Kran,' said Campbell looking yet again at her suicide note. 'She doesn't exactly confess to it. She says: "I hope my tip off last night stopped the contamination of more land…. I did it for my dad." If you read them together, the "it" just refers to the tip-off, nothing else. Don't you think she would have confessed to the attempt she made on Kenneth Kran's life separately?'

'She said "it" wasn't enough,' said Jenner rubbing her face with a cleansing wipe, 'to balance the wickedness she'd done to Sheena, her father and her mother. Surely that refers to her attack on Kenneth Kran. After all, she must have thought she'd killed him.'

'Don't you think she would consider that killing their murderer would balance the books without her needing to take her own life?'

'No, not really, Inspector.'

Campbell watched Jenner fold the tissue into a paper bag and put the car key in the ignition.

'Don't you think,' she asked, 'Christine tipping us off about the dumping was to keep us busy while she tried to kill Kenneth Kran?'

'So why didn't she just kill herself at Kenneth Kran's office after attacking him?' asked Campbell.

'She might have been happy with killing him. She might have only thought it inadequate later. She might have wanted to die in the peace of her own home.'

Campbell heard and felt the engine roar without moving him from in front of Ruth Pleasance's bungalow.

WDC Jenner was wrong. He knew it. The pressure of the tide was off his mental sluice gate. Alec Gowan would not return. As far as the efficiency expert was concerned the investigation was over with the death of Christine Pleasance. A trickle of river water could escape into the Wash of his brain: Campbell had a suspicion that Kenneth Kran's murderer was still alive. Murders could not so easily be ticked off in boxes along a clipboard. He still had a job and a source of ever flowing knowledge to tap.

'Detective Constable, please drive me to Kenneth Kran's office. I want to see how Mary Brown's doing.' Campbell stretched his neck and ankles, then said, 'On the way I'll snatch forty winks.'

Chapter 20

'Tell me, have you found anything?' asked Campbell. As he thrust his hands in his pockets he caught his elbow on the forensic van door. There wasn't much room with Mary Brown spreading her overalled body across the jamb. He watched her twist her pen in her cherub-like lips. She looked at her logbook and then back at him.

'What do you think I've found?' she asked.

'That's not a scientific way of going about things,' complained Campbell. 'I can only guess.'

'There is a probability,' said Mary Brown, 'that your guess might be right. This can be measured against the facts that I find – what I call the "Sniff Factor".'

He knew he would have to go along with Mary's new game to get the information he wanted, but he was really too tired for it. He mustered his strength. 'You've found something to link Kenneth Kran with the murders of Graham Pleasance and Sheena Kiljames,' he suggested.

'Might have done,' she said, dangling a plastic bag with a hair in it. 'Long, black and shiny,' she added.

'From Sheena Kiljames?'

'Very possibly.'

'And what about Graham Pleasance?'

'There's a whole shed full of tools Kenneth Kran could have used for doctoring the bridge. I'm having them bagged up now to see if I can find traces of the wood on any of them.' She paused and said, 'Campbell, there's some other reason you're here, isn't there?'

'Aye,' said Campbell. He could see from her expression that she was expecting that answer. She'd been testing him. There was a hint of satisfaction about her, which told him she'd discovered something else. He found enough space to sit on the floor of the van leaning his weight on his hand. The ridged surface was uncomfortable but, at least, it was a resting-place. 'And what about paint?' he asked.

He saw mild disappointment flick across her face until she spotted his hand.

'That's cheating,' she said. She grabbed his wrist before he could tuck it away. 'I'll have a scraping of that just in case we find any in there.' She nodded at Kenneth Kran's mobile office.

He tried to keep still while she scraped off the dried yellow paint he'd used on his back bedroom wall from his fingers. She scratched a little harder than was necessary, he thought. Afterwards he took his hand back and hid it in his pocket. He felt suitably told off. 'I didn't mean that sort of paint,' said Campbell.

Her small nose wrinkled. 'Alright Campbell, I'll give you a hundred percent on "Sniff Factor".' She picked out a carefully labelled plastic bag. Flakes of red colour lay in the bottom. 'How did you know?' she asked.

'Artist's paint?' he asked.

'I'll analyse it back at the lab. But I can tell you it is water soluble.'

'Where was it?'

'In the little kitchen they used for making tea. The materials we found in there could have been used to make the deadly cocktail. We've let the hospital know, and they are making a full analysis themselves. I'll keep you informed.'

Campbell fingered the tear in his pocket notebook caused by the fight between Bonita Arlotte and Christine Pleasance. Kinera Kran had caused that fight by sending Christine the letter about Bonita and her ex-husband. This middle-aged woman liked twisting around people's lives. He thought if he were asked to liken her to an animal he would have to say a snake.

It was time to pay a visit to the artist's house.

The driver's seat in front of Maggie finally clicked forward. She wanted to be free of her metal prison. She was darkened by the shadows it cast about her. The car was stifling and the child needed her help. Why had the Kran woman and her son left her here? She wasn't a useless old woman. She pulled first at the handle on the door. It opened a window. Then she tried to pull a small hooked lever. Failing daylight fell in on her as the door swung open.

She climbed the bank putting on her cardigan and looked down at the River Sparrow. Her family had been given the name of the river they lived next to centuries ago. It was her real name not one taken from a husband who'd left her and taken her son. The river was her past and her present.

But it was empty. She rubbed her hot eyes and looked again. There was no child in the water and no one on the muddy bank. She shouted for Eira and Kinera Kran.

'We're here,' came a female shout. Maggie squinted in that direction. Pastel rays reached through the purpling clouds and touched the ground somewhere behind the sluice and the tidal river. The shadowed figure of Kinera was waving at her from the metal walkway running over the sluice. She was holding a handrail, which was supported by occasional thin metal uprights. Over her, like a rectangular bridge, dark green painted girders formed a gantry for the lifting of the water gates. Maggie could just make out a ladder built into the structure at each end.

Below Kinera the water gates reached from the depth of the river to a few feet above the water. Concrete supported the metal structures and clad the riverbanks around the sluice. On the bank on the far side there was a small brick building. It had a bright red door. The colour was matched by the life belt stationed beside it. Beyond, the sluice keeper's cottage stood with its back door open and the river authority land rover parked in the yard. Next to that Maggie saw a small lorry with a grab folded like a sleeping claw tucked between its metal sides. She guessed the sluice keeper must have returned and the lorry was something to do with building up the riverbanks so she turned back to the water.

The river below was darker than the sluice. It lapped and gurgled around the water gates trying to escape to the tidal river beyond. Maggie hadn't been this far down stream for years. The sluice had always frightened her, despite it being built to prevent another flood like the one that killed her father.

She could see her son, Eira, squatting down next to a grey shape up there. It didn't look much like a child. There was something sinister, something she remembered from the war, from the field where her mother died. No, she must be wrong. All this business at Sparrow Bank had put her on edge. It was a child huddled in a grey blanket.

At least he was all right, she thought, as she made her way along the top of the bank. Her foot slipped with her first step onto the metal walkway. The hard rap rang out across the two rivers. She barked her shin on the step. She looked up and saw Kinera glaring at her. Her note-writing neighbour stood between her and her son. Maggie hoped she hadn't frightened the child. Gripping the railing she walked carefully forwards. She could at least comfort him.

Kinera moved to one side to let Maggie pass. It took her a moment to take in what she saw behind the artist. There was no child in Eira's arms. It was a bomb. It came to Kinera's waist and was standing on its round base. Fins spanned from the cylindrical metal to the narrow end of the bomb's body. Its nose pointed towards the sky. A mesh of rope was wound around Eira fastening him to the bomb and the sluice, his mouth taped.

From behind, Maggie felt herself thrown against the metal walkway onto her stomach. She felt Kinera's fingers bite into her back and pull at her cardigan. She managed to turn herself onto her back to face her attacker. She kicked and scratched and tore at Kinera's clothing and hair as best she could until a small sharp knife cut the skin on her neck. She heard Kinera hiss in her ear, 'I'll kill him, your so-called son. Do as I say.'

'Where's the lad you said was drownin'?' asked Maggie realising why the life belt remained on its hook next to the sluice.

'There was no boy drowning, you stupid old hag,' said Kinera. 'And there's no point in shouting. The sluice keeper can't help you. I've seen to that.'

Maggie's strength melted as it had done all those years ago. The only way to be in control was to be alone, she thought.

She watched Kinera tighten the ropes around her and the bomb. She and Eira sandwiched the cold metal shell between them. The coarse fibres from the rope cut into her loose skin. She felt like an oversized parcel. And she wondered if Janet had finished delivering the post yet and if her cousin would realise she was missing.

Her son choked and wheezed at her. 'Set him free. I'm the one you hate,' said Maggie.

'No.' Kinera seemed to be admiring her work.

'Take his gag off then. No one can hear that can help. You said so yourself.'

Kinera stepped forward and ripped the tape from his mouth. 'It's done its job. It stopped him warning you.'

'I know about your past, Maggie Norrice,' said Kinera. 'All the people talk about your mother's death beyond Drain Farm: the aeroplane that crashed on top of her during the Second World War. This is her bomb. I got it from the wreckage.'

'The air-force cleared up all the bombs because of the munitions dump nearby and at the end of the war they took them away too.'

'Not all of them obviously,' said Kinera. 'There were always so many crashes to go to. This part of England was covered with airfields. Crashing planes was a regular occurrence. But you know that. This bomb though must've dug its way into the soft fen soil. It was just waiting for me.'

Maggie remembered the field where her mother had died: the wreckage of the aeroplane; bombs littering the field. 'How did you find it?' she asked.

'The fen soil is still shrinking with all this evil land drainage,' said Kinera. 'It throws up secrets of its past. I saw part of the shell when I was painting the daffodil field. I dug it up when the pickers finished. I've been keeping it for this.'

'I should have guessed you were up to something,' said Eira, 'when I saw your husband's lorry parked there.' His head gestured behind him towards the sluice keeper's cottage.

'I can drive all his vehicles,' said Kinera. 'I've always been involved in his business. I knew he kept some trucks near Drain farm. It was all too easy.' She pointed out the powered hand trolley at the far end of the bridge, which she'd clearly used to get the bomb into place. It wasn't very big but Maggie guessed it would be too heavy for one person to shift.

'Did you know what Kenneth was doing?' asked Eira.

'Doing? What's this doing?' returned Kinera.

'Polluting. Contaminating. Dumping.'

Kinera looked at the bomb. Maggie could see she was no longer listening.

'What are you on about, stirrin' her up like that?' asked Maggie.

'Nothing,' said Eira. 'Nothing that matters now.'

Maggie looked across at the sluice keeper's cottage, at its dark windows and the still land rover with the lorry parked next to it. Kinera snapped her gaze away from the bomb and went over to the cab. On her return Maggie noticed she was carrying a red fuel can and a blowtorch.

'Petrol,' said Kinera, 'to light you on your way.'

'Why us?' asked Maggie. It seemed strange that this woman was going to kill her and her son now they were together after all this time apart.

'I want a human sacrifice for when I set the river free. I hate its captivity. I always planned to get you, Eira Dublin, ever since I learned you

had a cottage in the village. You poison people with the food you make.'
Kinera kicked him. Maggie winced. She continued, 'And you, Maggie
Norrice, have seen me coming out of the Wet Goose late at night. I would
have come and got you, but I didn't have to. You fell into my trap – the
one I set for him. What luck!'

Maggie looked out over the river, past the sluice keeper's cottage and
across the empty fenland fields. A breeze got up and rattled the sparse
clumps of willow brush along the bank, and it whipped the tidal and non-
tidal rivers into a brown frenzy. Maggie guessed that the tide had started to
push up the river behind them and the sluice was shut. Large blobs of rain
started to fall, bouncing on the metal around them. She wondered whether
the rain would stop the bomb from going off, or whether it would make it
explode.

WDC Jenner stood next to the door in Kinera Kran's living room. She
was trying to get away from the heat of the stove. She watched Campbell
standing squirrel-like over his notebook until he spotted a paper lying on
the mat between the wooden box by the window and the fire.

She wondered why he was still scratching away at this case when a
matter of a few hours ago it had been finished with, all neat and tidy. All it
needed was Kenneth Kran to wake up and confirm what they had
surmised. She suddenly felt scruffy and she poked at her hair. The stifling
air and the long day had sapped her strength. If it wasn't for this Kinera
woman we could all go home, she thought.

OK, so things weren't quite right here. The door had been left open.
But this lot were cranky. Parnold had said so, in between describing the
physique of the Spanish occupant. It was obvious they'd all gone. Couldn't
Campbell see that? He'd mentioned something about red paint on the way
over here, but did that really link Kinera with the attack on her ex-husband?
She supposed it might.

Watching him flick over the paper and read it where it lay, she leaned
on the door.

'This letter is from a food manufacturer in answer to a complaint from
Kinera.'

'Is it from Eira Dublin?' she asked.

'No, from another firm.' She could almost see his mind working for a
moment before he said, 'I'm going to look upstairs.'

'Do you want me to come?'

'Stay here in case anyone comes back.' He straightened himself and went through the stairs door.

Goodness knows what he was looking for now, she thought, hearing tapping sounds. At first she thought it was because she was leaning on the door. Then she realised that it was coming from the direction Campbell'd just gone in.

'Everything OK?' she called up the stairs.

'Aye,' he replied.

When Janet Sparrow first woke she wondered how anyone could've crammed her into such a small space. But the tender outside edges suggested to her she may have been crushed in here by feet. As her senses came back to her she heard voices and then the lumping of someone climbing the stairs that formed the jagged ceiling above her. She tapped the door with her head.

Briefly dazzled by a torch she only heard a female shout of, 'Inspector Campbell,' in her ear. Her shock was relieved by these people responding to her knocking on the cupboard door. At last she was able to breathe freely and uncramp her large limbs.

She recognised her rescuers as the plain-clothes policewoman and the Scottish Inspector who'd spoken to Aunt Maggie. Now she could tell them about Kinera Kran's letters.

Once they'd helped her to a chair by the fire the Scottish Inspector squatted down in front of her so his face was lower than hers and said, 'Tell me what happened?'

Large globules of rain started to explode against the windows, distracting her for a moment. He seemed to want to know every detail from the moment she came over the bridge. She tried to tell him about the food complaints Kinera'd made, but he just kept saying, 'Later,' and what did you see then?'

Eventually she managed to tell them about the letters, but the Inspector didn't seem interested.

'Kinera Kran can be prosecuted for that, can't she?' she asked.

'Excuse me,' said Inspector Campbell, 'but I must use the phone. I believe I saw one upstairs.'

At last, WDC Jenner thought, Campbell was phoning the police station and arranging for Kinera Kran to be picked up. Having heard Janet

Sparrow's story she understood her boss's interest in this artist: the woman was disturbed.

With Campbell gone she moved forward to see how Janet Sparrow was faring when the door burst open.

'Saw your car,' said Mrs Elizabeth Sturning. Jenner recognised the landlady's twang. She watched her lower a hood from her yellow hair and shake the rain from her bright pink plastic coat. Her flapping sandals and feet were soaked. 'I know who has been breaking in the pub,' the woman rushed on.

'Who?' asked Jenner.

Mrs Sturning thumped down a thin silver chain with a locket on it. When she pulled her hand away Jenner saw that the ornate case had been opened showing, on one side, a photo of a blond toddler and, on the other, a picture of a much younger Kenneth Kran.

'I found it on the flat roof when I went to open me bathroom window this mornin' after me bath,' continued Mrs Sturning.

'How do you know whose it is?' asked Jenner.

'I've seen it around the old crow's neck. I've got kids, you know. I don't know what she's up to, but I want her arrested.'

Jenner went over to the stairs to call Campbell.

'Did you hear me?' asked Mrs Sturning.

'Yes, I did. I'm just going to call my senior officer.'

'I was going to see her about it earlier.'

"The blasted woman won't wait a moment," thought Jenner. "I want Campbell to hear this." She sighed with relief as he came down the stairs. But she was irritated that he wouldn't let her summarise Mrs Sturning's story. She couldn't believe that he wanted to hear the whole thing again.

'That's when I saw them,' said Mrs Sturning at the end of her repeated tale.

'Who?' asked Campbell.

'I saw Kinera Kran pick up Eira Dublin and that funny old cat woman from opposite. Well, I think it was her. Can't say I've ever seen her in daylight before.' From somewhere inside her pink plastic coat she brought out a crumpled straw hat for Jenner's inspection.

Janet Sparrow gasped, and Jenner looked at her.

'Sorry, love. She's your Auntie, ain't she?' said Elizabeth Sturning.

'She's my cousin,' said Janet Sparrow. 'Inspector, Kinera Kran sent Aunt Maggie terrible notes. That's why I came here. I wanted to see why she did such things. I smelt gin in the bottle. She wrote them when she was drunk. She hates my Aunt Maggie, Inspector.' There was pleading in her voice and Jenner saw the panic in her round face. She bent over to calm her, though her own heart was throbbing. She hoped Elizabeth Sturning had finished showing them her collection of lost items.

'Which way did they go?' asked Campbell. She wondered how he could sound so unruffled.

'I heard Eira Dublin mention something about phoning the police,' said Mrs Sturning. 'And then they went down the river authority road. Kinera Kran's car was parked there, the other side of the yellow gate.'

'Thank you, Mrs Sturning,' said Campbell, and he went straight out of the room. Jenner felt obliged to arrange for Mrs Sturning to look after Janet Sparrow before leaving. By the time she reached the car Campbell was already at the steering wheel.

Chapter 21

Maggie felt more curious than scared as she watched Kinera again leave her and Eira on the sluice tied to the bomb. Kinera stepped off the walkway, the rain pouring down her face and drenching her chestnut and grey hair. The weight of the water pulled Kinera's scarf off, and Maggie heard her shout,

'I want him back.'

Wondering what Kinera was going to fetch this time, Maggie tried to reach the can of petrol and the blowtorch at her feet. Perhaps she could kick them into the river. But she was too far away and she didn't want to jiggle the bomb because she wasn't sure how stable it would be after all these years. She felt it rub against her shoulders. Eira was struggling against his ropes.

'She's mad,' he said.

'She's had her heart torn out,' said Maggie. She felt a curious sympathy with her. 'Shouldn't you sit still,' she added.

'Probably,' said Eira. 'But I don't want to.'

'If you don't sit still you might die,' said Maggie. 'And I can't have that.'

'You shouldn't care about me, I'm not your son. You know I come from Ireland.'

'How do you know you're not my son?'

'You said you saw me on the bridge the night the car went in the river,' said Eira, 'but I was no-where near Sparrow Bank.'

'Where were you?'

'I was at home looking after my young children.'

Maggie was shocked: how could the man on the bridge look so much like this man without being him? And she was pleased: there was a new possibility: her child might have children of his own. 'What are your children like?' she asked.

My girl's five and my boy's seven. Their mother was away for a couple of days at the time. She's back now. But she's used to me not being there, so she won't miss me. She doesn't even know about the fishing cottage and they aren't expecting me in at work – I've taken a few days off.'

'Do the children sleep well?'

'Joe does. Hannah doesn't. She woke up that night. It took hours to get her back off to sleep. I read her a story and gave her a drink.' Eira's voice fell. 'But I wouldn't expect her to talk to the police for me, even if they would accept an alibi from a five-year-old.'

'I would,' said Maggie licking the rain from her face. The wet chilled her. She shivered. Eira Dublin was not the man on the bridge. She would have to accept he wasn't her son, and she'd been so sure he was.

The walkway rattled. Maggie looked up. Kinera slid as she came along the wet surface towards them holding a large plastic sheet and a red thermal flask. Kinera swore as she tied the corners of the sheet to the metalwork. But Maggie was grateful for the shelter.

'I need to keep the bomb dry,' said Kinera. 'I want it to burn well when the tide is at its highest.'

'What did you lose?' asked Maggie. She felt she could understand Kinera's madness. Only a short while ago she'd tried to hang herself.

Kinera slapped Maggie's face. The wet made it sting. Eira said, 'Leave her alone,' and got kicked. Before the pain had left Maggie's cheek Kinera had ducked out from under the plastic and gone back to the railings.

'I know I wasn't any good,' shouted Kinera across the river. 'But I didn't deserve it. It wasn't fair. Why did you take him from me?'

Maggie called to her to get out of the rain. Kinera's body softened. As she came back the wind changed direction and the plastic above them started to flap.

'We were young,' said Kinera taking a swig from her thermal flask. 'Kenneth was still at college. We married anyway. I gave up art school. He gave up nothing. Our baby, Daniel was two by the time his father was in his last year at college.' Maggie saw her look at Eira, full of hate.

'Kenneth is older than you,' she told him. 'He was doing his post graduate doctorate.'

'I'm not your husband,' replied Eira.

'Do you think I'm stupid? You're not here because you look like him.'

Maggie was puzzled. Surely there couldn't be another man who looked like Jon Norrice. The Scottish Inspector had said that could be the case. So could this woman's husband be her boy, or could he be the man on the bridge, or both?

'I had a son,' Maggie said. 'I named him Matthew. I came to lose him when he was only a few weeks old. I thought he was Eira Dublin here. I was wrong. I wanted to be right, as you do. But this man hin't poisoned no body, let alone children.'

Kinera grasped Maggie's cardigan and twisted it in her fist. 'Kenneth cheated on me. I know. He left me looking after our baby while he went and did what he wanted. I hate maternal instinct: the need to give all to the child. If you go with it you tear yourself apart. If you fight it you end up hating yourself. But through everything I still love Kenneth.' She let Maggie go.

The wind caught the plastic sheet, twisted it and hurled it away. Maggie felt the rain pour over her and the cold drips from the girders above fall on her neck. Petrol and a blowtorch would light anything. Kinera needn't worry about the bomb getting wet, she decided. Lightning flicked across the sky turning all she could see white and blue. Before long it wouldn't matter any-more who her son was.

Campbell couldn't wait for Jenner to drive down the river authority road, but he didn't have the car keys. When she arrived and chucked them through the window he caught them and started the engine.

'Open the gate,' he called out. He rolled the car the short distance to the opening of the sandy roadway while Jenner pulled open the yellow metal gate.

'The lock was broken,' she explained as she got back in the car. 'Filthy weather,' she added.

As she shook the drips from her arms Campbell thought that the English really had no idea when it came to bad weather. There was far more weather in Scotland. But this rain kept coming. Gallons fell from the sky, drenching the grass on the riverbank, sliding off onto the sandy road in front of him. At least on the hills of Scotland the rain would readily run to the burns.

'Should I call for back-up?' asked Jenner.

'Let's check out Mrs Sturning's story first,' said Campbell. 'You can see what there was in the way of emergency calls this afternoon. See if Eira Dublin phoned through or even Kinera Kran.'

He wished he hadn't elected to drive. He didn't like driving at the best of times. The wipers were thrashing across the windscreen and still he couldn't see the roadway in front.

As they hadn't come across a car he gathered that Kinera must have gone further down the track with her passengers. He remembered from viewing the area from the bridge that the roadway was too narrow for two cars to pass with the steep riverbank on one side and a ditch on the other.

One moment he felt the urgency of Janet Sparrow's fear for Maggie Norrice and would rush forward despite being blinded by the weather. The next, he would think how useless they would be stuck in the ditch or smashed into the bank and he would slow. He could see Jenner gripping the dashboard and talking into the radio as he leaned over the steering wheel.

She said, 'There hasn't been any emergency calls connected with this area.'

He was about to say to her to call for back up when a sheet of plastic landed on the windscreen. So instead he stamped on the brake. The car slued on the waterlogged track, first towards the riverbank and then towards the ditch.

Maggie watched Kinera pour gin into the cup from her red thermal flask and drink greedily. She was completely soaked and sure she would soon be dead. She could accept that totally as the decision had been taken away from her. It gave her a freedom she'd never felt before.

'My father drank,' said Maggie. She raised her voice against the weather. Since she'd broken her silence and spoken to that Scottish Inspector she found she wanted to talk. 'He said it was because my mother died. Before that, he said it was because she weren't faithful. And before that he just drank.'

She looked towards the spewing water, no faces looked back.

'You knew my husband.' Kinera addressed Eira, Maggie noted. So she hadn't heard what she'd said.

'Not really,' he replied. 'I had some business with him, but I found out he cheated me too.'

'Cheated me too? Cheated me?' yelled Kinera. 'What do you mean?'

'You said, he cheated you,' said Eira.

'I blame him. I've always blamed him. But it was me who killed Daniel not him. I drank. Like your father, Maggie Norrice, I liked drink. I laid in a drunken stupor in the other room while little Daniel helped himself to the bleach.' She thumped the bomb. Maggie felt the metal ring against her back. Her flesh jumped expecting the vibration to turn into an explosion. But nothing happened.

A dark calm came across the sky. It was broken by a lightning flash in the direction of Hillvill. At the same time Maggie thought she saw a movement in the yard at the sluice keeper's cottage.

Campbell heard Jenner count to ten out loud slowly as they scrambled out of the ditch.

'Ten miles away,' she said.

He looked at her.

'The lightning,' she said.

She was only as wet, dirty and scratched as himself, he thought. She shook her radio. It was dead. He knew help would have to wait.

Through the gloom and the rain he could make out a car parked in front of them so he clambered up the bank. He could see the sluice straddling the river and the sluice-keeper's cottage on the far side with a land rover and a lorry parked outside. There would be a phone there and he knew the sluice would have a walkway across it. When the lightning flashed again, turning the sky to indigo, he saw figures on the sluice. Jenner started counting. She only got to five before the thunder crashed.

'It was close that time,' she said.

Mud sucked and oozed in his shoes as he made his way along the bank with Jenner following. The rain came in bursts now – sometimes as hard as hail, other times misty. He knew they'd been seen long before he reached the sluice because the standing figure was facing him. There was a stillness about them he didn't like. His instinct told him to stoop as he walked. A small figure was less threatening than a tall one. He gestured Jenner to do likewise. By the time they reached the walkway across the sluice the storm had moved on.

In the grim light he could see that the standing figure was Kinera Kran. He was amazed that she'd let them get so close without saying something, just a matter of yards from her.

He looked at her. She glared back at him. He searched her gaze. He tried to penetrate, soak up her fear, absorb her hate, check her violence. She turned away and touched something secured behind her.

'She's got a bomb,' whispered Jenner. 'Dublin and Maggie Norrice are there too.'

A distant flash brought back his dream: the tidal wave, the people in the car with him, looking up through water and surviving. It had nothing to do with coping, like Garden had said. It was an image explaining the way the fens were. They were below sea level. Except for the system of drains and pumps they would be under water. It was a delicate balance that kept the fenland people able to breathe below sea level. It had been a sorting dream after all. And now Kinera Kran intended to reverse the history of the fens. She wanted to swamp the lands.

'Mrs Kran,' called Campbell, 'This gesture is pointless.'

'It isn't,' she replied.

Campbell watched her come closer. He could see she was a woman with a mission.

'Mrs Kran,' he said. 'Your husband's in hospital. He's dangerously ill.'

'No,' screamed Kinera.

'He's been poisoned,' said Campbell. 'You can't help him like this.'

'Go away,' she wailed.

When she stopped for breath he said, 'Let them go, Mrs Kran.'

'Eira Dublin lent his cottage to Graham Pleasance so he could meet my husband there,' she complained. 'Graham planned to kill Kenneth.'

'I didn't know anything about it,' said Eira, bewildered. 'Sheena must have given him a key, but she wouldn't have been involved in a murder plot.'

'Who can tell what she did now,' said Campbell sadly. The villagers, he recalled, had only heard the splash of Graham's car going in the river and the roar of the other car leaving the village. This confirmed that the drivers must have already been in Sparrow Bank before the incident.

'I saw Graham tampering with the bridge one night on my way home from seeing the children at the pub,' said Kinera. Campbell saw her pause and allow her face to loosen.

'You're lying,' said Eira. 'Graham Pleasance wouldn't have done such a thing.'

'Aye, I think he would,' said Campbell. 'He'd become obsessed with his work, obsessed with Kran. For Graham, Kenneth Kran had become the embodiment of evil. He felt he could not be freed from his hate until he'd killed Kran.'

'When I heard the car go in the river, I thought Kenneth had died,' said Kinera. 'But I didn't get a visit to tell me he was dead. I didn't know what to do. I'd let it happen. For a while I'd wanted him to die because of Daniel.'

'Daniel?' asked Campbell.

'My son. But I know it wasn't Kenneth's fault at all.'

'Mrs Kran, Kinera,' said Campbell trying to catch her wandering attention. 'Graham Pleasance went into the river, not your husband.'

'Kenneth came to see me the next night and tripped over Maggie Norrice by my door,' said Kinera as if to herself. 'He told me everything. That stupid Graham Pleasance thought he was doing some wonderful thing by killing Kenneth. Saving the environment. What a fool! Graham Pleasance even told him about the bridge. He thought he had him secure, but my husband's an aggressive man. He over-powered Graham Pleasance and gave him the death that he'd arranged for Kenneth. You want to ask that goody-goody wife of his, Ruth. She knew something.'

Campbell imagined he saw the inside of the fishing cottage with the large Graham Pleasance and the strong Kenneth Kran struggling together among the wellingtons and coats. Graham Pleasance got the better of Kenneth for a moment and told him the death he'd planned for him. Then he was knocked out by Kenneth and placed in the driver's seat of his car. Kenneth must've straightened the place too because the grieving Eira Dublin had not noticed anything changed in his little cottage. Having lined the car up with the damaged part of the bridge Kenneth set the automatic car in drive and allowed the River Sparrow to fill it with water and kill Graham Pleasance.

Even now the river looked dark, as if it could swallow more lives and still remain unchanged, thought Campbell. 'What about Sheena Kiljames?' he asked. 'To you she was only a scientist working with Graham Pleasance?'

'I told Kenneth to get rid of her. She was another environmental evangelist. She was as dangerous as Graham Pleasance. I told him I would deal with Eira Dublin and Maggie Norrice. He recognised Maggie as the woman who saw him on the bridge that night and when he came the night after to tell me about it.'

Campbell tried to assess the situation. Kinera Kran looked tired, but overpowering her on the wet sluice could be dangerous. Maggie Norrice had said nothing. He could hardly see her as she was tied to the far side of the bomb. He wondered how much more she could take. Eira Dublin was a strong man, but that was of no use to him at present.

'Let them go,' he tried again. 'You are only making matters worse for Kenneth.'

'I can take my revenge. I can set the rivers free.'

'You look tired, Mrs Kran,' said Campbell. 'With rest everything will look different. You have your paintings. Everyone understands how you feel.'

'Sir,' whispered Jenner in his ear. 'There's someone else on the bridge.'

So Maggie's silence had not been a sign of weakness, thought Campbell. By not speaking she hadn't attracted attention so Kinera hadn't turned round to see a shadow moving along the walkway from the far bank towards her. He guessed it was the sluice keeper. For a moment he wondered why he hadn't helped earlier as his land rover had been parked in his yard next to the lorry since he and Jenner'd first arrived and seen the group on the sluice. But, perhaps, Kinera'd knocked him out or locked him in a cupboard and he'd only now managed to get out.

A clang rang out behind Kinera. She looked round as her blowtorch rolled past her into the river. Campbell knew he'd lost any chance of talking Kinera out of this, so he darted forward to grab her. But she'd already climbed around the bomb on the handrail avoiding contact with Maggie Norrice. She knocked down the small dark haired man in his sluice keeper's uniform sending him sprawling across the walkway. Campbell followed her past the bomb, Maggie and Eira. He stepped over the sluice keeper. He could just see Kinera Kran making towards the far bank. But before she reached it she climbed the ladder to the top of the sluice.

The evening sky was darkening again. The girders formed green angular shadows against the purple sky. As he climbed after Kinera he could see Jenner on the other ladder on the side he'd just left. He had to allow Kinera a way off of the sluice, so he called to Jenner to go back down. When he reached the top rung he saw Kinera crawl across the winding gear to the middle of the sluice. Then she stood up.

'No!' he called. 'Don't do it. Jumping solves nothing.' Looking down he could see Jenner had gone back to untie Eira Dublin and Maggie Norrice with the help of the sluice keeper. Campbell looked at Kinera. She stared at him. There was no life in her eyes.

Lightning cracked across the sky. Campbell ducked out of instinct. When he looked up, less than a second later, she was gone. He expected to see her body draped across the concrete base of the pillars supporting the sluice. But she was not there. A movement on the bank told him she'd taken the escape route of the far ladder. He followed going back the way he'd come. He noted that Jenner, who was nearer to her than him, had seen her too and given chase.

Campbell slithered past Eira Dublin and the sluice keeper helping Maggie Norrice off the walkway. As he moved his tired aching body along the bank he wondered why she hadn't escaped on the other bank when she'd had the chance. Just in front of him Jenner lunged at Kinera and pushed her over. They rolled down the slope into the muddy river's edge. He slid after them and told Jenner to release the woman beneath her. Tugging at Kinera's arm he tried to pull her away from the water, but she hung back. He looked into her face and saw a hollow madness in her eyes. She hadn't tried to get away because she still wanted to blow up the bomb, but now even that thought seemed to have left her.

'Come on,' he said. 'Nothing can hurt you now.' He watched her nod with the willingness of a mind gone completely blank.

Jenner scrambled up on the other side of Kinera. Campbell was grateful that she'd seen the change in their charge and was encouraging her to the top of the bank as he was.

Police cars littered every available space around the sluice. Campbell called to Jenner to find a car.

'Surely it's all finished now, Sir,' she said.

'Not quite.' He caught himself sighing with relief that the victims of the sluice and their aggressor had been taken safely away to hospital. Then he wondered if his sigh had sounded to Jenner as if he was cross with her. He was really too tired to care anymore.

It took five minutes before he spotted her waving him across to a police car parked by the sluice keeper's cottage. Somehow they'd found themselves on that side when the sluice had been sealed off by the bomb disposal squad.

Once seated, Jenner started the car. Campbell leaned his head against the backrest. 'Mrs Pleasance,' he directed.

'You don't believe Kinera Kran, do you, Sir?' asked Jenner.

He didn't reply. Such things had to be checked out. Until every lead had been taken to its natural conclusion his job was not done.

'Bonita Arlotte was Kenneth Kran's attacker,' said Campbell, stretching his knees and neck. 'Not Christine Pleasance. I thought it might be his ex-wife because of the paint – that's why we went to her cottage, if you remember? I expect Parnold's picking Bonita up about now. I used the phone in her room to contact him while you were looking after Janet Sparrow.' He mulled over with some pleasure how he'd come to this conclusion. Janet Sparrow had told him about the shawl in Bonita's room and it hadn't been there when he'd looked around upstairs. So he'd phoned the taxi firm and spoken to the driver. He confirmed Bonita had returned. Campbell'd guessed the rest: she'd attacked Janet and shut her in the understairs cupboard. Bonita was clearly stronger than her size suggested. She'd taken her shawl and gone back to the station. Well, OK, that was the easy bit. He already knew she was capable of violence. But it had tied in so well with everything else he knew about her. He took out his notebook. It was still as sodden as Jenner and himself.

'Run us home first,' he said. 'I'll get changed and Margaret will lend you something.' As she changed direction he fingered the tear in the paper.

'I was so distracted by Alec Gowan I couldn't think straight,' he explained. 'Look at my notebook. Her name appears everywhere, but I didn't notice it until it was torn. She was at the pub the night Graham Pleasance was murdered. You told me that yourself. But I didn't hear you. I was too busy chasing Christine Pleasance and talking to Maggie Norrice. When I did realise I'd forgotten that she hadn't told me herself about being in the pub the night Graham Pleasance died. By the time I'd got around to painting my back-bedroom I'd already assumed she'd told me about being in the pub because she'd told me she was with Kenneth Kran. I might have twigged the discrepancy if I hadn't been so busy thinking about Alec Gowan.'

'Not saying she was actually in the pub hardly amounts to a lie,' said Jenner.

'Bonita Arlotte adored Kenneth Kran, and she was jealous of Christine Pleasance's involvement with him. You should have seen the two of them scrap. She had every reason to try to murder him. She is a passionate woman who puts great store in her sexuality. She might even have thought she was doing it for Kinera.'

'And how,' asked Jenner, 'could she overpower a man like Kenneth Kran?'

'Come, Detective Constable, sex can be a dangerous game. There is a cruelty about Bonita's games. I have no doubt she can play as dangerously as anyone.'

'Hmm,' agreed Jenner.

'She had a peculiar loyalty to her patron, however. The attack on the post woman was opportunistic but she did it for Kinera.' He twiddled his thumbs.

'And?'

'I have every reason to believe our good Mrs Brown will come up with some finger-prints in the kitchen of Kenneth Kran's office. Bonita was more passionate than careful.'

Jenner laughed and Campbell allowed himself a whisper of a smile.

Chapter 22

Parnold stretched his neck as he approached the shawled shoulders and long black hair of Bonita Arlotte. He could hear WPC Garden scurrying to keep up and he was aware of the crepe-soled feet of Alec Gowan some distance behind. Unlike Campbell, Parnold thought, he welcomed the chance to be seen to be doing his job.

He took a deep breath. He would not allow Bonita to use her sexuality on him. It would not be easy to arrest her but that was his job. He'd been surprised when Campbell'd told him his findings on the phone and that he, Sergeant Parnold, was to arrest her for an assault on Janet Sparrow. When his boss had also said he thought Arlotte had poisoned Kenneth Kran he'd felt deceived. He'd seen Bonita's hips, her eyes, her hair – not a lying attacker of an over-weight post lady and her friend's ex-husband.

Campbell was a strange boss. Parnold fingered the handcuffs. You could never get inside his mind, rarely guess what he was going to say. He seemed friendly, easy going sometimes – almost too gentle to be a policeman. Not like Detective Inspector Pleasance had been. He'd treated his job like a religion. The law had been sacred and he who broke it had taken justice from him. When Parnold had first met Campbell he'd thought him stupid and slow compared to Pleasance. Campbell always had a list of tedious jobs that needed doing. Everything had seemed more exciting with Pleasance. Yet Campbell was so often right about people. You couldn't ignore that.

He looked at Bonita. A year ago he would have wanted to thank her for trying to kill Pleasance's murderer, now he didn't. His duty was to bring her to trial.

The small city airport receded from him as he made the arrest. WPC

Garden held Bonita's elbow as he cautioned the Spanish girl and handcuffed her. For a moment he allowed himself to glance at her face. He found her neat features twisted by hate into an ugliness that would one-day stay with her. He saw the smooth olive skin on her bare forearms and wondered what it would look like when she'd been in prison for fifteen years.

He congratulated himself on the legality of the arrest. Alec Gowan stood a short distance away. Parnold could only guess, with delight, at all the ticks he was putting on his form.

The creamy living room of the Pleasance bungalow had its brocade curtains pulled against the night. Campbell felt the heat of hastily turned on radiators to warm the rain-chilled air. Table lamps and wall lights made pools of light. Jenner stood outside of these by the door while Campbell sat on the deep chair he'd used on his first visit to see Ruth Pleasance.

He muttered some pleasantry about the change in the weather and how the strawberries would indeed be crushed. He paused and said, 'Kinera Kran has been hospitalised.'

'Should I know her?' Ruth Pleasance turned her blotchy, tear-stained face away. 'I have lost everybody, Inspector. Why should I care about someone I didn't know?'

'You met her at the seaside years ago. You had a beach hut near the Krans'.'

'Oh,' said Ruth Pleasance rubbing her hands together on her beige skirt. 'Such a long time ago, Inspector. Is it important?'

'The past is always important. We may not want it to be, but it defines our present and, if we let it, can dictate our future.' He leaned forward and lowered his voice. 'Your husband took out a second mortgage on this house. Christine mentioned it to us.'

Ruth Pleasance sucked in air, her whole body shuddered. 'We were going to take a holiday.'

'When?'

'The day after he died.' She looked towards the settee and quickly away.

Campbell rose and took two strides to peer over the back of it. A pair of bulging suitcases stood there. Silently he cursed himself at being taken in by this feeble looking woman.

'They weren't here when I came to tell you of your husband's death?'

'They were in the bedroom.'

'Are you still going away, Mrs Pleasance?'

'Yes, after the funerals.'

'You knew what your husband intended to do that night, didn't you, Mrs Pleasance?' said Campbell.

She shook her head. But he wasn't convinced, so he said, 'Graham was perfectly capable of making Kenneth Kran's death look like an accident. What your husband didn't realise was that things have changed quite a bit since he left the force. We have a different head of forensic now. She noticed the bridge had been tampered with. If he'd succeeded in killing Kenneth Kran he would have been found out.'

A tear leaked out of the corner of one of Ruth Pleasance's eyes.

Campbell pointed to the cases. 'And this wasn't holiday at all. It was an escape plan. You should have told us. Kenneth Kran would have been an immediate suspect. Other people have died because of your silence.'

'I'm sorry. I'm sorry,' she gasped between sobs. 'My husband was dead. I didn't want his name soiled with any criminality.'

From her pouting face he knew she meant her name, not his. As the victim's wife she could have looked forward to sympathetic neighbours in this Close of neat flowered bungalows. As the knowing wife of a man who attempted to murder another man and, instead, got himself killed, the local people would consider she deserved less than nothing.

'Because,' said Campbell, relying on his Scottish accent to lay the facts coldly before Ruth Pleasance, 'you tried to protect your own life-style, you lost your daughter. She thought she was the cause of your husband's death.'

'I know,' wailed Ruth Pleasance. 'I'm sorry.'

'So sorry you were going to take a holiday?' said Campbell with intense curiosity.

'I had to get away.'

Campbell wondered if there was enough evidence to arrest Ruth Pleasance for conspiracy to murder. Perhaps, 'Sorry' was enough. It had not been said under caution and there were no witnesses to her actions. Could this woman cope with carrying the guilt of an unpunished crime for the rest of her life? He looked at her. Despite the toughness under her shy exterior he could see the damage his words had done. He doubted that she could manage any more than a desolate existence.

'Goodnight, Mrs Pleasance,' he said walking through the door Jenner had opened for him. He would make his report and let others decide.

*   *   *

Campbell sniffed the hot black tea and hoped it was strong enough to wake him while he listened to Mary Brown on the other end of the phone. He'd allowed himself a few hours snug against his wife's warm body, until the need to go back to his unfinished thoughts had pushed him out of bed.

He put the phone down. Mary Brown wasn't particularly pleased that she now had to examine Graham Pleasance's tools for wood from the bridge instead of Kenneth Kran's.

Parnold sat on the other side of the desk, unslept and stroking his stubble. Alec Gowan stood behind him – glowing with reflected pride, thought Campbell. Steam from their coffee mugs danced in the early morning sun.

'The bomb disposal lot said Maggie Norrice and Eira Dublin were lucky,' said Campbell, stretching. 'I know I wouldn't fancy being tied to an explosive of that age. Kinera must have been mad to move it all the way round on the roads in that lorry.'

But Parnold looked eager to tell his news and he started to speak before Campbell had closed his mouth. 'Bonita Arlotte,' he said, 'confessed to poisoning Kenneth Kran at about the same time fingerprints matched her dabs to the ones on the bleach bottle in the office kitchen.'

'Did she say why she tried to kill him?' asked Campbell.

'Because of his carrying on with Christine Pleasance behind her back,' said Parnold. 'She went round his office to kill him. He was feeling down and he told her how his son Daniel had died: left to drink bleach while his mother lay drunk in another room. Arlotte said she knew he was lying about it being Kinera's fault. She knew he lied because of Christine. And then she knew how she was going to kill him. He liked his sex that way and when he was secured she nipped his nose until he opened his mouth. She said he passed out. Shock, I suppose. It probably saved him.'

'I see,' said Campbell with enough weight to point out that he hoped the confession was gained while adhering to the rules of questioning. 'At least Kenneth Kran will be able to pay for his murder and pollution if he lives. And if he dies I'm sure Ruth Pleasance will not be sorry.' Despite his words the result of the attack on Kenneth Kran still revolted him.

'Did Mary Brown confirm the black hair at Kenneth Kran's office?' asked Parnold.

'It's still being examined,' said Campbell.

Suddenly he wanted a bit of peace and quiet so he said, 'Let's see your report,' even though he knew full well Parnold hadn't had time to write one.

As his sergeant left he followed him out the door. Wadges of paper were everywhere in the main office being checked and double-checked. Campbell looked over the bowed heads and knew he mustn't disturb them. The murders of Graham Pleasance and Sheena Kiljames seemed suitably solved as well as Kenneth Kran's poisoning. He picked up his jacket and asked Alec Gowan if he could drive.

'I've been taken off your work study,' he said. 'I'm covering Sergeant Parnold now full time.'

'He's going to be writing that report for hours,' said Campbell. 'Come on.'

He noted how Gowan could walk almost normally without a clipboard in his hand, and inside the beard the man's face was sharp and his eyes bright. How ridiculous he'd been to allow himself to be bullied by someone's presence. Campbell knew himself. He was not like Maggie Norrice. She'd been physically abused; all this poor man had done was watch him.

'I need to see Maggie Norrice one more time,' he said to Gowan. 'I promised.' His promise to visit her made only on Sunday seemed a long time ago. He felt he'd let her down by not being able to prevent her being kidnapped by Kinera. Perhaps he could put that right by having a word with her about that long lost son of hers. He didn't feel he could relax until he knew who he was.

Chapter 23

Maggie Norrice had the door open. The cool damp air breezed through the tiny pump cottage and out through her open bedroom window. One of her cats sat on the doormat, another on the recently cleaned windowsill. She looked forward to Eira Dublin coming around later as well as Janet bringing her tea. He'd insisted he would always be her friend when he came back to her cottage with her from the hospital last night.

He'd sat under the bare bulb and shown her pictures of his family. His mother had been a small dark haired woman like Maggie, but with smooth gentle features, instead of her sharp angular bones. His father had been tall and like Eira except for his red hair. He had his birth certificate at home, he'd said, and these people were definitely his parents. It was very possible his blood was green.

Hours later he'd gone home, not to the fishing cottage. He would sell that now, he'd told her. He would go to his English family in their modern Norfolk house. But he would call back today, he would always come and see her.

The quiet measured footsteps the Scottish policeman made in her lane alerted Maggie to his arrival long before she saw him poke his head around the door. He stepped over the cat at Maggie's bidding.

'Alone today,' she remarked.

'Aye,' said Inspector Campbell. 'I've left my driver in the car. I wanted to check you were all right after last night.'

'It was Kinera's husband who I saw on the bridge that night, wasn't it?'

The Inspector nodded his head.

Maggie didn't think policemen usually took it upon themselves to care about victims, but he clearly hadn't come to arrest her so perhaps he could help her solve her problem now he was here. Despite all that had happened she hadn't found her son. Her past was incomplete.

She couldn't remember getting the scrapbook from the dining table drawer but it was already in her hands. When she passed it to him she said, 'I heard it said on the sluice last night that Kinera's husband looked like Eira Dublin. And Eira is the image of how my Jon looked the last time I saw him – if you allow for age. Could Kinera's husband be my son?'

'No,' said Campbell. She heard him soften the word for her. 'We know his background,' he explained. 'And we know a little about your husband Jon – his real name was Johan Stangarde.

'Oh.' She sat back down on her holed chair and looked at her cat-plucked brown trousers.

'Your son could still be alive somewhere,' said Inspector Campbell. 'People sometimes get the local press in the area they think loved ones might be to do an article about them. It sometimes brings results.'

'He could be anywhere,' she said. Watching Inspector Campbell turn the pages of the album she thought how important those papers had been to her. They'd survived the flood. They'd been all she'd had and she'd wasted so many years worrying over their contents.

Why had Inspector Campbell stopped turning the pages and why had his eyes stayed steady over one picture only? She knew by the thickness of the pages exactly where he was looking. He brought the page closer to his face, then pushed it away.

'Whose this?' he asked.

'My father,' she said. 'He'd just won that speed skating cup.'

He closed the book, handed it to her and left without saying a word. Maggie watched him go and clucked at her cat who'd been disturbed from his place by the door.

Campbell jogged down the lane. He usually liked to keep some energy in reserve, as he never knew when he might need it, but today he used it without thinking. Having passed his car he heard the door open, close and lock. By the time he got to the Wet Goose Alec Gowan's short but rapid thumping strides had brought him to his side.

As Campbell knocked on the door some of the blistered black paint peeled away.

'We're not open 'till twelve,' came the shouted reply. It was Harry Sturning's voice. At least he hadn't run off after the dumping incident on

Sunday, thought Campbell.

'What's going on?' asked Alec Gowan, wiping sweat from his forehead with a handkerchief.

'Observe,' said Campbell as he turned towards one of the windows. He thought he'd seen a movement in the bar so he held up his card to the glass and called, 'Police.'

'Oh, right, coming,' shouted Harry Sturning, his voice muffled by the closed window.

Campbell saw Alec Gowan was actually interested in what he was doing now he was denied tick boxes to try and fill. He even looked open to discussion. 'Have you written your report on me?' asked Campbell.

'Not finished.' Gowan looked embarrassed. Campbell noted that the reddening of his cheeks under his whiskers was not only due to the indiscretion of discussing his work but also because the tone in which he'd said it told Campbell that the report would not be a good one.

The door opened. Harry Sturning slicked his hair back with his hand as he let them in.

Campbell said, 'Good morning,' and noted the man's blood-shot eyes.

Leaving the door ajar the publican took them through to the kitchen. 'Liz is in town,' he said, his London accent cutting through the stale beery air to Campbell. 'She's taking the kids to school and doing some shopping.' Harry Sturning sat them down at a small table covered with a plastic cloth. Campbell took the chair on the side opposite to Sturning while Alec Gowan sat between them.

Campbell noted Sturning's fingers trembling as he held his coffee cup and wondered if the drink was laced with alcohol.

'It's cooler than Sunday – the last time we met. The storm Monday night cleared the air,' said Campbell.

Sturning examined his coffee.

'We took a knife off you on Sunday,' said Campbell almost casually..

'Yes, it was my old man's,' said Harry Sturning. 'They sent it to me from Canada when he died. I'd like it back, Inspector.'

'Your Dad gave it to you?' Campbell was delighted at the reply. 'Did you say he was from Canada?'

'No I didn't, but he was from Canada. But why the interest in my old dad?'

'What was his name?' Campbell could see Alec Gowan watching first him and then Sturning as each of them spoke.

'John Sturning,' said the publican.

'Not Johan Stangarde?'

'Then I would be Harry Stangarde, wouldn't I. And I'm not.'

'Sturning, Stangarde,' mused Campbell gently. 'I'm only guessing but these surnames are very similar.' He took out of his pocket the picture he'd got from the prison record of Johan Stangarde, alias Jon Norrice, and laid it on the table.

Campbell watched the publican. Harry Sturning turned the picture to face him. He looked calmer now. His pale, veined skin was flushed but steady. He was drawn instinctively towards the photograph.

'Dad looks so young in that picture,' said Harry. 'Where did you get it from?'

'Police records,' fabricated Campbell.

'That figures, the old scoundrel died in prison over in Canada. I've got two other pictures of him.' Sturning turned towards the sink. Campbell watched him carefully. He knew he couldn't trust him. But he could see beyond the pile of washing up lay an old leather wallet. Harry Sturning brought it back to the table and pulled out two black and white photographs. The first one showed a man in his sixties with thin grey hair and lips sucked into a toothless mouth, which caused his jaw to form a large square dominating his face. Even so the eyes shone out with smooth confidence – as they did in the second picture. Campbell recognised this one. It was the same image as on the photograph Maggie Norrice had given him.

This man was Jon Norrice. Harry Sturning was Maggie Norrice's son.

Campbell reflected on how he'd thought Maggie Norrice's son might have been involved with the murders of Graham Pleasance and Sheena Kiljames; and how he'd wondered at the normality of a child brought up by a vicious criminal.

He was about to ask him about his early years when he heard a scuffle at the back door and remembered the black and tan dog outside. He was coughing with discomfort at the memory of being cornered in the yard by it when he noticed the publican's waxed green coat hanging behind the door. The dog whined and scratched.

'Shut-up,' yelled Harry Sturning.

Then Campbell saw two pairs of men's wellingtons among the jumble of shoes and boots by the doormat. One pair was black and clean; the other was green with thick dried mud around the souls and up the sides. The top of the green boot nearest him was falling away from the bottom where a tear nearly separated the two parts.

Realising Harry Sturning had followed his gaze to the boots and was now looking at him Campbell tried to cover his thoughts. He remembered Mary Brown's pride at the fight Sheena Kiljames had put up for her life. The Chinese-Irish girl had lashed out with her sickle, catching her own boot. Could she have caught her attacker as well? And the night Graham Pleasance was killed, although it was certain Kenneth Kran murdered him, hadn't his car been parked over this way? Perhaps that was one of the reasons Graham's plan had failed. Maggie had seen Kenneth caught in the security light at the front of the pub. Yes, Harry Sturning had known Kenneth Kran much earlier than just from that night of the surveillance on the industrial site, as he'd said. He was almost certain now that Harry Sturning had driven dumping lorries on other occasions before last Sunday even though he'd said it had been his first time. Even with Kinera telling her husband to get rid of Sheena Kenneth need not have done the deed himself.

'How did you know where Sheena was?' asked Campbell.

Sturning got up from his seat. Campbell did likewise. The square shaped publican reached among the washing-up and drew a small sharp serrated knife from among the dirty crockery.

'Mr Kran told me she was at the bird sanctuary. Took a letter of hers from Dublin's cottage. Pleased as punch he was.'

Campbell was about to try and shove the table into him when Harry Sturning moved to one side and wrapped a large arm around Alec Gowan's neck. He pulled the small bearded man towards the door to the passage leading to the front of the building. Before he reached it a small grey haired lady in a shabby pink cardigan and brown nylon trousers appeared there. Her dark questioning eyes looked across at Campbell from the doorway.

'Why did…?' she asked and stopped.

Maggie Norrice felt herself being pulled across in front of the steely bulk of the man with the knife. She could see the bearded man who'd looked after Janet the day she'd found out her son might be alive. He had been shoved into the Scottish Inspector, who'd shouted at her, 'Get out, Mrs Norrice,' but now was saying, 'Harry, No.' She wasn't quick enough to respond to the Inspector's warning. The man with the knife had swapped hostages – the bearded man for her.

Being gripped so tightly was suffocating but she was wary of the knife. The cut on her neck from Kinera's blade was still sore. But she was without fear. She felt empty of emotions. She'd faced death at her own hand and by someone else's already. Her only aim now was to do what she thought was right for others.

She watched, feeling helpless, as the unbalanced bearded man toppled Inspector Campbell into the kitchen table, knocking it over. The coffee mug rolled across the floor. The left over drink spilled over some old photographs, which were too far away for her to see clearly. The leg of the table caught Inspector Campbell in the chin.

She saw him fall backwards just before her body was propelled down the front passage to the open pub door. She felt Harry, as the Inspector had called him, behind her: breathing, swearing. His voice sounded curiously familiar. The roughness and violence of his movements made fifty odd years ago seem like yesterday. He loosened his grip slightly to try Inspector Campbell's car door. She knew better than to try and escape.

'Try the other side of the bridge, Harry,' she said. She knew the chance of finding any cars in the northern part of the village was smaller than if he went in the other direction where there were more houses and the church. More people could get hurt if Harry went south. Anyway, it was all she could think of to delay him, to allow Inspector Campbell time to catch up. She hoped Harry was panicked enough not to think through what she'd said.

They reached the centre of the bridge before she heard Inspector Campbell shout out, 'Harry, stop!'

Maggie felt herself twizzled round to face the Scottish Inspector as Harry stopped.

'Don't kill her, Harry Sturning,' said Inspector Campbell. 'She's your mother.'

'I don't have a mother.' The deep voice of her captor passed directly from his chest into Maggie's.

'You do, Harry Stangarde, Harry Sturning, Harry Norrice.'

What was this Inspector Campbell saying about her being this man's mother? Surely it was just a trick to get him to release her. Her disbelief fought with the sensations of familiarity she was getting from this Harry Sturning.

'Norrice, Stangarde, Sturning?' she asked.

'Shut up,' said Harry Sturning.

'Did your father tell you that you had no mother?' asked the Inspector.

Maggie looked down at the shape of his forearm braced against her and the black hairs curving over his pale skin. They moved as she breathed.

'She died when she had me. You can't trick me like that. This is just some old woman.'

'Matthew?' asked Maggie Norrice.

In reply he crushed her within the vice of his solid arm. But she could feel his confusion. She hadn't seen him on her night-time ramblings. She'd seen his wife at the window drawing curtains. She was much younger. This man seemed too old to be her son. But she could smell stale alcohol on his body and fresher stuff from his mouth. Her father had aged before her eyes with alcohol. Could he really be Matthew?

'Harry Matthew Sturning?' asked Inspector Campbell.

'Yes,' he replied.

'Your father lied to you,' explained Inspector Campbell. 'It was he who nearly killed your mother before he ran away from arrest. He took you with him. Did he look after you?'

'That's none of your business.'

'I would have cared for you, if he hadn't taken you,' said Maggie, still unsure of whether this man was her son or not, but it was a gambit the Inspector clearly thought would work. Then Maggie felt sadness flow through her captor and the grip of his arm about her chest and neck weaken. 'I wouldn't have let any harm come to you,' she said. She could tell he wanted to believe it, but she wasn't sure if she wanted to. He let go of her and slumped to the ground. She could see him properly now. She recognised him. He was bigger all round, but he was like her father with his dark hair and dark eyes.

'You had blue eyes,' she protested.

'My daughter was born with blue eyes and blond hair,' said Inspector Campbell walking towards her and her son. 'By the time she was a few months old they'd turned brown. By the time she was ten her hair was the colour of old oak wood. My son looked like my wife's father when he was born, but now he looks like my brother. Children change.'

She put both her arms about the desolate figure sitting on the bridge. And she cried with sorrow at what her son had become and relief that she had found him. Her past slipped away from her.

The shadow of Campbell over them made her look up at him. He was sliding the knife away from where her son had let it drop. Matthew's rough face scratched at her cardigan and she felt the dampness of his tears soak through to her skin. She loved him. She always loved him. And she always would.

Campbell spotted Alec Gowan limping out of the pub towards them as he arrested Harry Matthew Sturning, born Matthew Norrice. And pondered for a moment the sign above the pub door. If Harry Sturning had been the licensee and not his wife his middle name could well have been up there.

'Thank you,' said Alec Gowan. Campbell noted his relief at seeing Harry Sturning in handcuffs. 'How did you guess he was a murderer?'

'Things are rarely as they seem, Alec.' Campbell was surprised he could use the man's name almost with ease. 'Every unknown needs to be delved into before the truth is revealed.'

'Policing looks different when I'm not actually filling in a form,' said Gowan. From his voice Campbell could tell the efficiency report about his work would now be a glowing one.

'Some things you can't measure,' said Campbell. 'Mary Brown calls it, "Sniff factor".'

'What's that?' asked Gowan.

'How much you can work out before the facts prove it for you.' But Campbell could see by the efficiency expert's face that he would always try to measure the immeasurable.

The End

OTHER TITLES BY THIS AUTHOR

SMOKE SHADOWS (Inspector Campbell Mystery No 1)
by Pamela St Abbs paperback and e-book

TWISTING TIDE (Inspector Campbell Mystery No 3)
by Pamela St Abbs kindle e-book

THREADS OF TREASON by Mary Bale paperback, large print
hard back and e-book

ABOUT THE AUTHOR

Pamela St Abbs lived in Norfolk for most of her life. She now lives in
Scotland with her husband. She also writes as Mary Bale when writing
about her eleventh century detectives, Abbess Eleanor and Therese, Abbess
Eleanor's protégé.

www.ingramcontent.com/pod-product-compliance
Lightning Source LLC
Chambersburg PA
CBHW060427130626
46555CB00005B/2245